'Where the hell is Dave?'

He took a deep b_____ _____ _____ see three feet throug_____ _____ Further down. He pu_____ _____ his throat burned, b_____ _____ scythed upwards, and_____ _____ face he was screaming _____ _____

Something moved, g_____ _____ murky water. He could barely breathe but that didn't matter. He swam over to it. His hand grabbed at it – got a handful of material. Then he was on his way up.

'I've got him,' he sobbed. 'I've got him.' Ryan swam over to him. 'Here, take him off me,' Paddy said. Suddenly there was no strength in his arms and legs, and he had a terrible thought – what if Dave were dead. What would he say to Donna? But he couldn't think of that. He doggy-paddled over to the rescue boat, the best he could do, and did his best to help Tony haul first Dave and then Ryan out of the water.

He grabbed on to the side of the boat but there was a sudden swell and he drifted under its upthrust prow. Another sudden surge drove him upwards. He felt his head hit the boat, and a split second later a tremendous pain lanced across his skull and right down his neck. He grunted in surprise and lost his grip on the boat.

# SOLDIER SOLDIER

## DAMAGE

**Sarah Jackson**

CENTRAL

BOXTREE

First published in Britain in 1995 by
Boxtree Limited,
Broadwall House, 21 Broadwall, London SE1 9PL

10 9 8 7 6 5 4 3 2 1

A CIP catalogue record for this book is available from
the British Library.

ISBN: 0 7522 0755 5

Cover design by Shoot That Tiger!

Cover photographs by Central ITV show Gary Love as
Sergeant Tony Wilton, Jerome Flynn as Cpl. Paddy Garvey
and Robson Green as Fusilier Dave Tucker.

Typeset in Sabon by SX Composing Ltd, Rayleigh, Essex
Printed and bound in Great Britain by
Cox & Wyman Ltd, Reading, Berkshire

# Acknowledgements

Thanks to:
M. Barnard; Kimberly Borrowdale; Judi Fleming;
Marty Fouts; Lavina Galbraith; Averley James; Ben
Jeapes; Peter C. Johnson (Major US Army Reserve);
Tristan Kirby; Jay Knox-Crichton; Andy Lane; Mike
Lowery; Pandora; and Alexander van Thorn for all
the help, though all errors and sins of omission are
mine alone. Thanks also to all the usual suspects —
including the rest of the Roadtrip — for all the usual
reasons. You know who you are.

# Prologue

After Bosnia, Germany was heaven. Paddy Garvey stood ramrod-straight, between Tony Wilton and Dave Tucker, on the parade ground at Muenster, waiting to receive his UN medal. They were part of a short line of men that included Company Sergeant Major Stubbs and Captain Voce, who had been chosen as representatives of the entire batallion. The other men would get their medals later.

Colonel Jennings made his way down the line, followed by a private carrying a tray of medals, as the band thumped out a slow march. A camera flashed. Paddy couldn't tell if it belonged to one of the journalists or to one of the small cluster of wives seated off to one side.

Joy Wilton was there, of course, and Marsha Stubbs the wife of the company sergeant major.

But not his Nancy.

There was no-one there to take a photo of him, no-one to be proud of him.

He'd gone off the rails when she'd left him. She'd wanted her career more than him. He'd nearly wrecked his own career because he couldn't cope without her. Well, he'd pulled back from that particular disaster, even thought he'd found someone else.

Then the posting to Bosnia had come, and though Christina had said she'd wait for him, gradually her letters had stopped. He hadn't needed to be told she'd found someone else.

And now here he was back in Muenster, with a headful of bad memories – children starving, women dying under a hail of snipers' bullets, old men freezing on the streets – and only a medal to show for it.

Unless what he had been told unofficially was true. But he'd decided not even to think about that until it was confirmed.

Paddy suddenly realized he was grinning – and that the colonel was pinning the medal on Tony's chest. With an effort he made a poker face; then he noticed out of the corner of his eye that Dave Tucker was scowling.

Donna's not here, Paddy thought. That was just typical of her, and it would surely lead to yet another row between her and Dave. Yet for all that their marriage was rock-solid.

Whereas he and Nancy had seemed like the perfect couple and yet –

But there wasn't any time to brood. The colonel moved in front of Paddy, who saluted crisply despite the stiffness of his dress uniform. He was grinning again, but he realized that didn't matter.

Colonel Jennings shook his hand. 'Well done, Corporal,' he said.

Paddy muttered a thank-you, feeling as if he would explode with pride. The colonel took a medal from the tray, and pinned it next to Paddy's Northern Ireland medals. Then he was moving on to Dave, even as Paddy saluted again.

Then he'd finished and moved off towards the podium to give his speech. Paddy glanced at Dave, and they grinned at each other. Just at that moment Donna rushed in carrying Macaulay, and took her place next to Marsha. There was a tall black guy with her, carrying the pushchair. Paddy glanced at Dave again, expecting him to be furious; but he just grinned with a mixture of affection and resignation.

Colonel Jennings climbed up to the podium. The band finished playing. There was silence for a moment and then the colonel said, 'These UN medals are being received on behalf of you all in the King's Own Fusiliers. When I assumed command of this batallion on your return from the former Yugoslavia, your last CO told me you had turned in an excellent team effort in very difficult conditions.' He paused. 'There were also examples of individual bravery, of which we can all be proud —' here it comes, Paddy thought. It was a real struggle now to keep his poker face. 'This morning the Ministry of Defence confirmed that, in recognition of an act of outstanding courage whilst under sniper fire in Central Bosnia, Corporal Patrick Garvey of B Company is to receive the Queen's Gallantry medal.'

So it's true, Paddy thought. It is true. And not even the thought of how proud Nancy would have been of him could take the edge off it.

# Chapter 1

Cyprus, Paddy thought: sun, sea, sand and sex. Maybe they wouldn't have much time for sea and sand, or the opportunity for much in the way of sex – since Operation Lion Sun was all about some fairly heavy training – but just seeing blue skies above him and feeling the heat of the sun on his face made his spirits lift. He followed Dave Tucker and Eddie Nelson, the newest recruit to their happy band, across the airport tarmac away from the plane they'd arrived on.

Dave took his sunglasses out of the top pocket of his desert combat uniform, and put them on. He nodded to the RAF flight attendant, a beefy bloke with a brick-red face. 'Nice flight,' he said, in a fake posh accent. The man stared back blandly, and once they'd gone past Dave added in his normal voice, 'Shame about the stewardesses.'

'I thought he was going to thank us for flying Crab Air,' Eddie said. He'd only joined the King's Own a few weeks before, and though he had started late – he'd been a copper before – he'd fitted straight in.

Paddy reached across and took Dave's glasses off. No point risking the wrath of Tony Wilton this early in the proceedings. 'Give the lad a break, boys,' he said. He tucked the glasses back into Dave's top pocket. 'I thought he was quite tasty, myself – '

'Oh yeah – ' Dave started.

At that moment CSM Stubbs shouted from behind them, 'Nelson! Tucker!' They all looked round. He had a clipboard in his hand, and he was standing next to Tony Wilton. 'Baggage party,' he said, gesturing at the belly of the plane.

Eddie and Dave ambled over to him.

'Any time this week'll do,' Tony said.

Paddy grinned and left them to it. As he walked away, he heard Dave grumble, 'I thought the baggage was down to the boys in blue – fly the friendly flag and all that.'

'As usual, you have been horribly misled,' the CSM said quietly. Paddy knew that tone. Any minute now, he thought. 'Now MOVE!' the sergeant major bellowed right on cue.

Paddy grinned. Rank had its privileges, after all.

The facilities at Bloodhound Camp were a bit basic, but then the place was used strictly for training. Paddy found his bunk, one of a dozen or so in a clapboard barracks that was surprisingly cool after the pounding heat outside.

He emptied his kit into his footlocker then went to get cleaned up for dinner. He was hot and sticky from the flight, and though he liked the heat he knew it would take him a few days to adjust – not that he was likely to be given them.

The shower block was a long building made of corrugated iron that looked even older than its fifty odd

12

years. Inside, there were rows of sinks, most of them in use. He stripped to the waist then found a spare place. The water was so cold it made his teeth hurt. He soaped up quickly, then rinsed off even faster. Even so, Dave and Eddie walked in before he'd finished.

'All the comforts of home,' Dave said, staring around the room.

'Dunno what you're complaining about,' Eddie replied. 'You aren't going to be missing out on much from what you said.'

Dave shrugged. 'You should be so lucky,' he said.

They're up to something, Paddy thought. I don't want to know, I just don't want to know.

He splashed some more water on his face. Dave grinned and turned on the tap nearest him. 'Marvellous,' he said. 'Cold and cold running water.'

Paddy looked up. He could feel the fine hairs on his arms and back standing up with the cold. 'You should see the bogs,' Paddy said. He'd made a brief diversion there, and regretted it almost immediately.

'Let's hope the chef's not too keen on curry,' Eddie said.

Thank you for that, Mr Nelson, Paddy thought. He shivered, but realized his face still felt sticky. He slooshed some more water over himself.

'Paddy,' Tony Wilton's voice said. 'Company Office.'

At least, that's what Paddy thought he said, but it made no sense. Puzzled, he straightened up slowly.

'Want to turn the hearing aid up,' Tony said.

13

Paddy turned. Tony walked into the room. 'I said, Company Office.' He sounded a bit pissed off, but that was typical Tony – throwing his weight around while he got used to a new situation. Mind you, he hadn't been best pleased at having to leave his wife, Joy. Paddy didn't blame him for that. She was pregnant with their second child, and if Tony could have found a way to stay with her, he would have. Paddy nodded to him. He grabbed his towel and dabbed at his face.

As he left the room he heard Dave say, 'How's your room, Anthony? We haven't got a seaview, and we've complained to reception –'

'You should have spoken to me first,' Tony said. 'The manager's a mate of mine.'

Paddy grinned as he pulled his jacket back on. Tony was okay as long as nothing challenged his authority. He'd settle into the new situation soon enough. They all would.

Paddy cinched his belt and tugged the jacket down smartly, wondering why the Company Office wanted him. Briefly, he considered going back and asking Tony, but he knew that with the sergeant in his current mood it would get him sarcasm at best and a tongue-lashing at worst.

Paddy stood at attention in the Company Office, waiting for Brucie – Lieutenant Forsythe – to acknowledge his existence. A man bustled in with a box of papers. Somewhere, a phone rang. Come on, come on, Paddy thought at the officer, but he was careful not to let his impatience show on his face. The lieutenant looked twenty-three going on seventeen, and Paddy knew enough about officers to realize that the less experienced they were, the more likely they were to lash out at anything that even appeared to challenge their authority. It was no wonder the lieutenant had picked up his nickname. Not that he even knew about it, Paddy presumed.

Eventually, Brucie stopped what he was doing. He retrieved a long white envelope from his desk drawer and held it out to Paddy. 'Some bright spark at BFPO forwarded this to Bloodhound early. It's been sitting on the camp warrant officer's desk for the last two days.'

Paddy took it. 'Thank you, Sir,' he said. He already knew what it was – he'd recognized it as soon as he saw it – but he slit it open with his thumb anyway. You had to hope.

'Hope it's not urgent, Corporal,' the lieutenant said. He had already turned away, his attention on some important files or other.

'No, Sir,' Paddy said. 'Just my divorce papers.'

Brucie grinned, perhaps in embarrassment. 'Yes, well,' he said. 'Not as if it's a big surprise, now is it?'

That's the British Army for you, Paddy thought as he went through the motions of being dismissed. Sensitive as a brick shithouse.

So that's it, he thought as he left the office. Nancy gone. Nancy gone forever. He'd known it for a long time, of course; but now it was official. Now it was down in black ink on white paper and he would just have to stop hoping – because for one moment when he'd looked at the page he'd flashed on the idea that it would be from her, not the solicitor, saying she had changed her mind after all.

Tony was talking to a group of men outside, saying something about a barbecue that evening. Free booze, courtesy of the OC.

Well whoop-de-roo, Paddy thought as he walked straight past them. Whoop-de-bloody-roo.

Tony came up beside him. 'What is it, mate?' he asked.

As if you don't already know, he thought. He just scowled at the smaller man. 'Later, Tone,' he said. He picked up his pace, and just for once Tony took the hint and let him be.

Left to himself, Paddy would have given the barbecue a miss; but he knew it would have created a bad impression. Besides, if that twerp Brucie – or worse, Major Voce – got wind of why, they'd have the Padre down on him faster than you could say decree absolute. And since he was there, he supposed he ought at least to pretend to enjoy himself.

Besides, the smell of meat slowly roasting over charcoal was delicious. If you had to be bloody miserable, he supposed there were worse places to do it than on a beach in Cyprus with a cool sea breeze on your face and free beer to drink with your mates.

He turned and realized that CSM Stubbs was watching him. Stubbs was a tall man, but the marine colour sergeant standing next to him was even bigger, and powerfully built with it. He had skin the colour of coffee with the merest trace of cream in it, and he carried his bulk with the coiled-spring grace of a big cat. His face held all the expression of a stone idol.

Stubbs said something to him. Paddy thought he heard his name being mentioned, but couldn't be sure – whatever it was, Stubbs was almost smiling, though. But the colour sergeant's expression didn't change.

So that's Colour Sergeant Ryan, Paddy thought. He'd heard rumours before they'd left that he was the hardest bastard they were ever likely to come up against. Looked like the rumours might just be true.

'Cheer up, Pad,' Dave said. Paddy turned, just in time to catch the can of lager Dave lobbed to him. 'At least we've got local leave to look forward to.'

'You have,' Paddy said gloomily. 'What's the betting Forsythe'll draft me into adventure training?'

Dave grinned. He pulled the tab on his can. 'That's the trouble with you bachelors,' he said. Thanks a bundle, mate, Paddy thought, but before he could say anything, Dave continued, 'It'll only take a couple of days – and look at it this way, while I'm being dragged round the shops by Donna, you'll be living it up in the fleshpots of Paphos – ' he added gloomily.

'I suppose,' Paddy said. He took a pull on his lager. It was warm. He wondered how many more people Dave had told about Donna coming over early, against regulations.

' – Mind you,' Dave went on, brightening up. 'By that time even my Donna might have seen the inside of enough shops to keep her happy – '

Stubbs was watching them. 'Keep it down,' Paddy said. 'You keep stumm about Donna. If the OC finds out about her being over here ahead of the posse, he'll go ape.'

'No chance,' Dave said. That probably meant he'd only told half the batallion. 'She's nothing to worry about, what with Joy looking after Macaulay back in Muenster. I've told her not to phone.' He glanced meaningfully over at Stubbs. 'Besides, I'm not the only one who'd be for the high jump – ' He drained his can.

'Dave, for pity's sake,' Paddy said. 'Just because she roped Marsha Stubbs into coming with her doesn't make it all right. And God knows what Kelly'll get up to – '

'She's all right, my sister-in-law,' Dave said. He looked down regretfully at his can and swilled it around to check, but it really was empty. 'Just knows how to have a good time, that's all. Like her sister – '

Just then Tony came up. 'Gentlemen,' he said. 'We need two more for beach polo. Any takers?' Dave raised an eyebrow in Paddy's direction.

'Not me, mate – ' Paddy started.

But Tony went straight on. 'Right, that's you and you – you're on the Blue Team, got it?'

'Yes, Tone,' Paddy said. He knew better than to get in the way when Tony was doing his Gung-ho Sergeant routine. Something else to blame on Ryan, he supposed.

The game, once they got started, was good fun. Dave rode on Paddy's back, and they were soon in the thick of it. They downed one pair, then another, by hauling the rider bodily off his partner. Paddy stopped for breath. A knot of men over to the side resolved itself when the Blue Team pair crashed out.

'Just us now, Padders!' Dave yelled. 'Go get us some Greenies!'

There were two pairs from the Green Team left.

'Great odds,' Paddy yelled. 'Yee-argh!' He charged across the soft sand with Dave clinging to his back like a monkey. They rocketed towards their opponents, who were just a bit slower on their feet.

Make that one, Paddy thought. He slammed into his opposite number. They locked, shoulder to shoulder. The onlookers – all half a dozen of them – roared. Paddy felt Dave swing round and grapple the other rider. For a second he thought Dave was going to slide off. He shifted his grip on Dave's legs.

Dave shoved the other man in the chest and he toppled back, taking his partner with him. The crowd cheered. Paddy waved to them and turned towards the officers – the marine colour sergeant among them – to wave again, as Dave said, in a phony TV broadcaster voice, 'There was a question mark over their fitness but I think – '

Something slammed into Paddy's backside. He stumbled forward, arms flailing. Dave yelped. Paddy thudded shoulder first into the soft sand, with Dave next to him.

The crowd jeered and laughed. Paddy rolled to a sitting position. Winded, he shook his head to clear it, then looked up. Eddie and his partner were punching the air with glee.

Great, Paddy thought. Great end to a great day, Garvey. Can't even win a bloody game of beach polo. He got up, scowling, and realized that CSM Stubbs, Major Voce and the marine colour sergeant were all looking at him.

'Good bloke, our Nelson,' he heard the CSM say. The colour sergeant scowled.

Paddy turned away in disgust. There'd been a time when he'd have been the one they were talking about – Paddy Garvey, the all-singing, all-dancing soldier with the unblemished record and a fine career ahead of him. But that had been before Nancy left him and he'd gone off the rails: he'd put himself back together he'd thought, but not until he'd nearly wrecked his career – he'd taken a tank without permission and damn near killed Tony with it – and only sheer luck and the intervention of Major Voce had saved him from being booted out altogether.

Well, those days were over, but so were his days of being the platoon high flyer, for all Major Voce had said if he did well in Bosnia he'd be considered for sergeant.

Queen's Gallantry medal or not, he hadn't said anything since.

Well, to hell with it.

He scrambled to his feet and went over to where the others had clustered round Tony. The sergeant swigged from his bottle of Pils. 'That was a definite foul, you two handsome gentlemen,' he said. 'Remount.'

'What for?' Eddie said.

20

'You took them from behind,' Tony said. 'You're not allowed to take them from behind.' He made a suggestive thrusting movement with his hand.

Like a big kid, he is, Paddy thought. And this was just like some playground argument.

'Since when?' Eddie demanded, like the world would end if they didn't win.

'Since I'm referee,' Tony said, tapping himself on the chest. He waved his bottle around. 'I'm god and my word is final.'

Christ, Paddy thought. He's feeling sorry for me – that's what this is about. Bloody hell – I get my divorce papers and he thinks winning beach polo's going to make it up to me.

Dave, of course, didn't see it like that. He pushed Tony and Eddie apart and peered through the gap. 'Thank you,' he said. 'Come on –' he looked at Eddie.

'Sod off, Tone,' Paddy said. 'We don't need any favours.' He started to walk away. 'We lost, didn't we?'

Of course they'd lost he thought as he strode off down the beach away from everyone else. They'd had him on their side. How could they have won?

After a bit he found a good place to sit. He stared out at the sea. It was like looking in at himself: a vast coldness inside him that nothing could warm. He scooped a pebble up and threw it in the water, but when it hit he couldn't hear the splash for the lapping of the waves on the shore. He heard people approach – Tucker and Nelson, maybe others – and sit down on the sand.

21

A mouth organ began to wail. Eddie, all right, Paddy thought.

Probably scared I'm going to top myself, he thought, only half joking. Sooner or later they'd come over and try to cheer him up, but he didn't want to be cheered up, he wanted to think about Nancy. He'd wanted her from the first moment he'd seen her – maybe it was her laugh, or that impish smile – and she'd made him work damned hard to win her. First she wouldn't go out with him. Then, when he'd asked her to marry him, she'd said no repeatedly. But faced with the prospect of being left behind when he'd been posted to Hong Kong for two years, she'd changed her mind. He'd been so sure they were forever. When she first got her permanent posting to the SIB, he'd been behind her all the way. So proud of her – his wife, the suddenly high-flying military policewoman. And then suddenly it was all too real – she'd been offered training back in England that would have seen her promoted over him.

And the world had come crashing down around him.

He could have stood being away from her that one time. He might even have learned to handle the ribbing the other lads gave him over it. But he knew it wouldn't end there. She'd want to take it further – go for her officer training, put off having kids till it was too late, all of that.

He picked up another stone and hurled it hard at the water. Maybe he should have realized that if Nancy had a career, he wouldn't have everything he'd dreamed of – but that without her, he had nothing at all. And maybe he should have followed her to London and dragged her back. Or even left the army to be with her . . .

Maybe, maybe, maybe. His life was full of maybes, and just because he'd managed one short-lived relationship since Nancy left him didn't mean he had stopped wondering about them. He picked up a large pebble and started picking imaginary bits of sand off it.

Somewhere behind him, Eddie's mouth organ wailed on.

He felt a hand on his shoulder. Dave. He hadn't heard him come over.

'Here we go,' the Geordie said. He pointed out to sea. 'Solve two problems in one go. I do a bunk and start up as a fisherman.' He grinned. 'And you marry Donna and take the flak for her being out here early.' He stared out at the sea, all fake romanticism.

Paddy pretended to think about it for a second. 'No, it'd never work.'

'Why's that?'

'You'd never catch any fish,' Paddy dead-panned. He supposed he was just going to get on with it – and that meant letting Dave and Eddie cheer him up, if that was what they wanted to do.

Eddie's harmonica stopped. He came padding over. 'The guy in the taverna was on about the local brandy,' he said.

Paddy could see what was coming. 'Was he really?' he asked. He turned the stone over in his hands.

'Yeah,' Eddie said. 'I fancy a bit of it – might be our last chance for a while.'

Last chance for what, though, that was the question, Paddy thought. 'Leave off, Nelson. You know what you're like – ' Eddie looked hurt. Paddy smiled to soften it a bit. 'You've only got to look at the label – ' It wasn't going to work. He knew it.

'Yeah, I'll come in on a whip around,' Dave said.

'Oh don't be a prat, Dave. We've an early start tomorrow.' He played his hole card. 'I don't want to be on the wrong side of that big sod of a marine, even if you do.' Mind you, he thought, no matter what they did staying on Ryan's right side was going to be tough.

Dave trumped him. 'Horatio can sort him out.' He nodded towards Eddie, who didn't look best pleased at the prospect. 'Come on, Paddy,' Dave cajoled. 'After all, you do have something to celebrate.'

Celebrate, Paddy wondered. Well, he supposed that if he'd been married to Donna he might think the divorce was worth celebrating. To hell with it. He could always call it a wake, anyway. After all, something had died inside him when she left him. 'Oh all right,' he said. 'Sod it. I'm in.' He reached into his pocket for cash for the whip.

Eddie pushed his hand away. 'No, no,' he said. 'You can get the next bottle – that is, if you're still standing.'

Oh Christ, what have I done, Paddy thought, but Eddie was already walking away.

'Good lad,' Dave said, and followed him.

Bad news, more like, Paddy thought.

He threw the stone at the sea.

One whiff of alcohol and Eddie Nelson was anyone's. By the time the pickup truck arrived to take them all back to Bloodhound, he'd single-handedly sunk three quarters of a bottle of brandy. Two of the local ladies of the night had had to be surgically removed from round his neck, and he'd had to be physically restrained from doing a strip-tease to a bouzouki version of 'Hey Big Spender'.

Paddy, on the other hand, was nicely mellow. Nancy, he had decided, was a lovely dream, nothing more: now it was time to wake up and live the rest of his life.

Tony Wilton appeared on the verandah. 'Last call for Bloodhound,' he shouted. He clapped his hands. 'Get your arses moving.'

He was standing by the steps leading down to the road. The only way to get to the truck was to go right past him.

Paddy downed the last of his brandy. He surveyed Nelson, who was sprawled across one of the tables, and Dave, who was chatting to one of the local girls as if he'd never even heard of the clap, never mind having had his own very special close encounter with it.

Paddy sighed. 'Come on, Dave – let's get sleeping beauty here home,' he said.

Dave stood up. He smiled at the girl.

'Come *on*, Dave,' Paddy repeated. He hauled Eddie to his feet and hooked the man's arm round his neck.

Dave did the same on the other side. 'I think she likes me,' he said.

'Likes your wallet,' Paddy answered as they hauled Eddie towards the steps. 'You were bloody lucky Donna didn't find out about that time in Hong Kong – don't push your luck.'

'Thank you very much, Padre,' Dave said.

'Yeah, well – ' Paddy started.

'Nice one, Paddy,' Tony cut in. He walked along-side them as they went to the truck. 'OC gets wind of this, he's going to go apeshit. You're supposed to be his section commander.'

Fine, Paddy thought. First I'm the bloody padre then I'm a nursemaid. 'Yeah well I'm not his bleeding keeper, am I?' he demanded. 'It's not down to me, Tone – ' He put out his hand to forestall any sarky comments. Besides, it gave him a second to figure out what to say next. For some reason, he was having a bit of a hard time thinking straight. 'He said he could handle it.' He pushed Eddie's arm from round his neck and walked – *very* steadily, he was sure – to the truck.

'You know he can't,' Tony said from behind him as he clambered up to the tailgate.

Paddy looked round, sure there was a good answer to that, but not quite able to figure it out; but just at that moment Eddie toppled over and landed at Tony's feet.

Dave winked at Paddy. 'Don't worry about Hora-tio,' he said quietly to Tony. 'He's going to sleep like a baby.'

That man, Paddy thought. That man has a plan.

He did, too. They didn't tell Horatio about it, though. They let him find out about it when everyone else did. That was the next morning, when he woke up in his bed. Stark naked. In the middle of the parade ground.

# Chapter 2

The trouble with some mornings was that they started too early. The first day of training was one of those days, Paddy thought as he waited for the briefing on the Fibua exercise with the rest of the platoon. It was only nine hundred hours, but the sun was brighter and hotter than noon on an English summer's day. Out of the corner of his eye, he saw Eddie gulp down water from his canteen. At least he had *some* sense. But not enough. The state he was in, he was going to be in trouble – or cause it, Paddy thought furiously. But even as he thought it, he knew it was at least partly unfair. He'd let himself get so caught up in his misery over the divorce that he'd gone along with yet another one of Dave's stupid schemes when he should have known better. Well, he was probably going to pay the price for it just when he should have been proving he was sergeant material.

Major Voce arrived and, after taking over the briefing from Lieutenant Forsythe, began to speak: 'Your task is to clear targets one, two and three of enemy personnel, then secure the whole village. Now, for the old and the boldest among you – you know who you are –' his gaze drifted across the group,

' – you'll have done Fibua exercises in Germany and Hong Kong till they were coming out of your ears. But for some of you new lot, it'll be your first chance to operate in a hot climate.' He stared directly at Eddie, who looked as though he were about to throw up at any minute. 'So, be aware of the terrain, be aware of the dangers, and follow the rules. Good luck.'

He handed over to Tony, who moved up front and centre. 'Right,' he said. 'Collect your ammo. Four mags per man. Radio check in five minutes.'

Here we go, Paddy thought. 'Section One, ammo point!' he bellowed. Most of the section, including Dave, moved out immediately. Only Eddie was left behind, following more slowly and looking a little bewildered. 'The dead arose and were seen by many,' Paddy said. He glared at Eddie thinking, one of those mornings? Going to be one of those days, all because the stupid sod couldn't look a bottle of brandy in the eye.

'I'm all right,' Eddie muttered.

'I don't think so,' Paddy snapped walking past him to catch up with Dave. He'd seen stretcher cases that looked more all right. 'Dave – keep an eye on him. Fire support him only, got it?'

'Changing the orders already,' Dave said, sounding affronted, as if he were the least likely squaddie in military history to do something he shouldn't.

'You got any better ideas?'

The Fighting In Built Up Area exercise took place in

the ruins of a village on the steep side of a hill. The cottages — mere roofless shells, most of them — formed a maze of ochre-coloured walls and piles of stone that stood out in stark contrast to the emerald of the grass. Gunfire rattled out all around. Paddy and his section squatted down behind a drystone wall, awaiting orders. Above them on the hillside, another section defended one of the cottages. Between them, Tony and Lieutenant Forsythe co-ordinated the attack. Somewhere off to the west a thunderflash exploded and a cloud of smoke billowed up into the clear sky.

Paddy glanced back at his men. They were ready for it, he thought. Only Eddie was still a worry, trailing along at the end. Give Dave his due, he was doing his best to help the bloke keep up — but it wasn't going to be enough. Not with Ryan on the prowl.

'One Section,' Forsythe called. 'Right flanking!'

Game on, Paddy thought. 'Right lads,' he said. 'Prepare to move.'

They trotted up the right side of the hill while Two Section laid down covering fire. Paddy's SA80, with the yellow blank-firing attachment clipped to the barrel, bounced against his hip. They were slow, he thought. Not just Eddie, all of them. Nevertheless, they made it past a single twisted olive tree and up to the next cover.

A narrow cleft that had once housed a set of steps led steeply up between two walls to the roofless remains of a cottage. They'd have to be quick — they'd be exposed while they clambered through the gap, and there was only room to go in single file. Beyond that cottage there were others, some with roofs, that would give an approaching enemy plenty of concealment.

'Delta fire team – move!' Paddy ordered sharply. The men nipped through and made it cleanly to the next cover. 'Follow me!' Paddy said, and led the other fire team through the cleft. As he did so, he realized that Ryan was observing them from behind the wall.

Paddy got to cover and turned just as the others caught up with him. Almost at the same time Eddie, the last man, swore softly. He'd got stuck trying to clamber through the gap.

'Give him help,' Paddy said to the nearest squaddie, Knox. 'Now!'

Knox ran back, doubled over, to haul Eddie up. Gunfire rattled from behind them. Paddy glanced back in time to see a couple of men dodge back behind the wrecked stone walls above them.

It's all right, he told himself. They weren't accurate – Eddie was on his way over, with Knox behind him. But Ryan reached out and grabbed him. 'You. Lie down,' he hissed. 'You're dead . . .' He shoved the man hard on to the ground. Then he turned to Paddy. 'Corporal, your section is holding up the rest of the platoon.' He ran off before Paddy could say anything.

Paddy sank back against the wall. 'Shit,' he muttered.

The word was hardly out of his mouth when Tony appeared. 'Paddy, what's going on?'

'That's one hard bastard,' Paddy said. He scowled

in the direction Ryan had taken, but the colour sergeant had already vanished into one of the buildings.

'Right now he's the least of your problems,' Tony said. He sounded disgusted. 'Hurry up.' He too ran off.

Got to pull it together, Paddy thought. Got to prove that one screw-up doesn't make a complete cock-up. 'All right,' he said aloud. 'We've got to put some fire down.' He looked at the men. 'Tucker. Nelson. Simple task. Get up there –' he jerked his thumb at the hillside. 'Smoke off the approach.' That should slow the enemy down, at least. The two men gawped at him. 'NOW!' he bellowed.

They went.

'Follow me,' Paddy yelled to the others. He led them onward. When they reached the next section of wall, he dared a look back. There were Eddie and Nelson – they hadn't had the wit to make sure they weren't sky-lined. A thunderflash arced up.

'What the bloody hell?' Paddy muttered to himself. The thing was going wild, almost thirty degrees off where he needed it. It dropped neatly into the open top of one of the buildings. A thick cloud of yellow smoke billowed up. About five seconds later Ryan stumbled out coughing, with his eyes streaming.

'Oh shit,' Paddy said for the second time.

After lunch, there was a weapons check ready for the afternoon exercise. While he was preparing, Paddy noticed Ryan talking to Eddie. From the look on his face, Eddie wasn't enjoying it one bit.

Nothing I can do about it, Paddy told himself firmly. He'd already decided the best thing to do was keep as far clear of Ryan as he could. Besides, it wasn't like Eddie didn't deserve a bit of a bollocking. He turned his attention back to what he was doing.

Dave was sitting next to him. 'Well look at that,' he said. He nudged Paddy in the ribs. CSM Stubbs was saying something to Ryan. Eddie got up and headed in their direction. He looked well pissed-off.

'What was all that about?' Paddy asked. 'Ryan – '

'Told me he wasn't one of the brothers,' Eddie said. He made a face like he'd tasted lemons. Paddy raised one eyebrow at him. 'I'm black and he's black, so he thinks I'm expecting special treatment – '

'You could have him for that,' Dave put in.

'Dave – ' Paddy said warningly. Whatever the rules said, they had to live in the real world.

'Well he could,' Dave insisted.

'Get real.' Paddy finished checking his weapon and turned to Eddie. 'Best thing you can do is get on with the job and keep out of the sod's way. Got me?'

Eddie nodded, and after that they finished the weapons check in silence.

A bit later, the platoon was called together for an exercise briefing. They sat on the hillside in front of Major Voce, who had Ryan and CSM Stubbs next to him. Tony and Lieutenant Forsythe were standing behind the men. Paddy could almost feel Tony's disappointed gaze boring into his back.

'Right,' the major said. 'As a result of your somewhat mixed success at attack – ' he stared straight at

33

Paddy, ' – the enemy have escaped. Recce reports show them reorganizing in section strength to the north.' He jabbed his fingers at Paddy. 'Now you shouldn't find that too difficult to believe, Corporal Garvey.'

'Sir,' Paddy said, striving to keep his voice and face expressionless.

'Pull your fingers out, gentlemen,' Voce said. 'Mr Forsythe?'

'Sir,' the lieutenant said. 'Sergeant?'

'Prepare to move!' Tony screamed.

The men clambered wearily to their feet. Screwed it up once, Paddy thought. Doesn't mean we have to do it again.

'Just think of the rest of the batallion, bored to tears in Muenster,' Dave said. 'Fighting over who's going to get the next round in.' He smiled cynically at Paddy. 'S'pose a spot of sunbathing's out of the question?'

Paddy shouldered his pack and his rifle, and let his helmet dangle in his hand. Bloody Tucker never did know when to stop. ''Fraid not, Dave,' he said. 'You've been booked for an audition.'

'Oh yeah?' Dave asked, walking right into it.

'It's for a film called "Garvey's Heroes" – '

'Marvellous,' Dave said. He struck a heroic pose with his SA80.

Good man, Paddy thought. 'You get killed just before the credits go up,' he finished drily.

Tony came up behind them. 'No he doesn't,' he said. 'I want him in my film – "Wilton The Bare-

34

Handed Strangler".' Dave made the mistake of grinning. 'Move!' Tony bawled at him.

Dave scarpered. Paddy made to follow him, but Tony said, 'Paddy – no more cock-ups, all right?'

'Don't worry, Tone,' Paddy said, keeping his voice neutral. 'Nelson'll be fine.'

'Oh, will he?' Tony asked, not even trying to hide the sarcasm in his voice. 'Who got him pissed then?'

It was too much. Paddy hefted his SA80 and squinted into the sun. 'Oh come on,' he said. Suddenly keeping on Tony's good side didn't seem worth the effort. It was a bit late for that, anyway. 'He knows he can't drink. He should have backed off.'

Pick a fight with Tony and you always got one. 'You're his section commander. You're meant to be looking after him.' Paddy stopped walking and rounded on Tony, but before he could say anything the other man went on, 'Tucker and Nelson got pissed last night because they were trying to cheer you up.'

Great, Paddy thought. It isn't enough that my wife isn't my wife any more. It isn't enough that today's all screwed up. No, everything everyone else does has to be my fault, too. 'Is that so?' he demanded, suddenly full of fury.

'Yes it is, you ungrateful git,' Tony said. He stalked off.

Paddy saluted to his retreating back. 'Yes, Sar'nt. I'll try to be a better person, Sar'nt.'

Like hell.


They slogged up one hill after another, with the dust

35

puffing up in little clouds as they walked. It might have been quite pleasant, except for the weight of their rifles, packs and canteens, and the discomfort of having to wear a helmet in the dry heat.

The enemy were somewhere in the hills that rose above them. Paddy led his section through the deep shadows cast by a clump of cypress trees. He motioned them to wait, then whispered to Eddie to recce ahead. As he did so, Paddy and Dave took up a position behind a large boulder someway ahead of the rest of the men.

Eddie halted behind an outcropping of stone. He motioned to them to wait, then looked at the hill through the telescopic sight of his rifle.

Do it, Paddy thought. Do us proud this time, Eddie. He wanted the man to redeem himself as much for his own sake as Paddy's.

'Look,' Dave hissed. 'Over the brow of the hill –' Paddy looked where Dave pointed. He couldn't see anything. 'Injuns!' Dave said. He grabbed a dry stalk of grass and stabbed himself in the neck with it. Then he rolled his eyes and collapsed sideways.

Paddy couldn't be bothered to conceal his disgust. He glanced at Eddie, expecting to see that he'd moved on; but he was still there, staring at the hill as if he thought it might disappear if he took his eyes off it.

Paddy scurried forward to him. 'What's up?'

'Just looking at the goats,' Eddie said.

Bloody hell. 'We'll stop and collect conkers, if you want,' Paddy said.

'No, look,' Eddie said. He gestured at the hill.

'They're all over the rest of the hill.' Yep. Goats, Paddy thought. A leg at each corner and grass in one end and out the other. Big deal. But Eddie pointed to the west flank of the hill. 'But not up there.'

Paddy squinted up at the hill. Eddie was right – and even as they watched, light glinted silver off metal or glass. 'Nice one,' Paddy whispered.

He ran, crouching, to check out the west flank, while Eddie went back to the others. He got some way forward before he saw the enemy – a whole section of them, occupying the roofless shell of a cottage. Gotcha, he thought and ducked back behind a tree.

He signalled to the rest of the section, then radioed in their position. The order came back to hold firm and observe.

Just wait, you beautiful babies, he thought at the men on the ridge. You're all ours.

A moment later, he turned to check on the men. Eddie and Dave were disappearing off into the bushes. Paddy sighed and ran back to the men.

Even before he got there, he heard the noise – a child's voice, gabbling something in Greek. He pushed through the bushes. Eddie and Dave were talking quietly to a lad of about seven. He was almost hysterical.

'What the bloody hell?' Paddy demanded.

Dave pointed at a plume of greasy black smoke that was billowing up over the ridge. 'Think the nipper's in trouble,' he said.

Paddy stared at the kid. It was just possible that he was playing a trick. But he was pale and shaky, and looking at the terror in his eyes, Paddy didn't think so. 'Okay,' he said. 'Okay.'

There was one good thing about only being a corporal – no-one expected you to make any really big decisions on your own. He clicked the radio on, and once communications had been established, told Tony about the boy.

'Hold your position, and await further orders. Over,' Tony said through a hiss of static. He signed off, and the radio went dead.

Paddy stared at the plume of smoke. He was tempted to send someone up to have a look; but if he did that he might give his section's position away to the enemy. That wouldn't be a problem if the boy was genuine, but if he was winding them up Paddy would have screwed the exercise for no reason and against orders. He glanced at the boy. Eddie had done a good job of calming him down, but he was still trembling and his breathing was fast and shallow.

He's in shock, dammit, Paddy thought. We ought to be doing something. As it was they didn't even have a blanket they could put round him.

Just then the radio crackled into life. 'Two-One Bravo this is Two-Zero Alpha,' said Major Voce's voice. 'Send sit-rep, over.'

'Two-One Bravo,' Paddy said, thinking, at least they're taking it seriously. He glanced at the boy again. 'The kid seems pretty genuine.' He paced forward and squinted at the ridge, estimating. 'We've got some smoke about a mile west. Over.'

'Two-Zero Alpha. Are you asking to suspend the exercise?'

Shit, Paddy thought. Just what he didn't want – the responsibility for making a decision. Yet he wanted that third stripe, and making decisions was what rank was all about. 'Two-One Bravo,' he said slowly. 'We're just ... assessing the situation. Over.' He wasn't going to get away with dithering for much longer, and he knew it.

There was a sound off to the side. He turned. Colour Sergeant Ryan pushed through the bushes. He stalked straight up to Paddy. 'Ignore the brat, Corporal,' he said without preamble.

'No!' Eddie blurted out. 'Colour Sergeant,' he added quietly and much too late. Ryan turned slowly and gave him a glare that could have frozen hell over. Eddie didn't back down an inch. 'He's really scared.' He put his hand on the boy's shoulder. 'Look.'

'Got a degree in child psychology now, have you Fusilier?' Ryan's tone was venomous. Eddie stared levelly at him. It was more than Paddy thought he could have done. The big colour sergeant turned back to him. 'You're adrift, Corporal,' he said. 'Get moving. Now.' He turned and walked away.

Paddy stared at Eddie. All his doubts crystallized in that moment. The kid was in trouble and they all knew it. He should say something. He knew it, but crossing the colour sergeant was asking for trouble. He was still gathering his courage when Eddie said, 'I've seen kids in trouble before.' Ostensibly he was speaking to Paddy, but they both knew his words were meant for Ryan.

Shit, Paddy thought. Can't let him get into this

alone. 'We've got some smoke, Colours,' he said. 'There could be a fire.'

Ryan turned back, still with his habitual sneer. 'You know what they do this time of year?' he asked, then answered himself. 'They prune the vines then burn the cuttings.' Not and make smoke like that, they don't, Paddy thought. But still ... he hadn't known. He felt his tongue move in the dryness of his mouth. 'It's up to you, Corporal,' Ryan said. 'You're a big boy. But if you get it wrong, don't expect any mercy from me.' He left.

Paddy watched him go. He took a deep breath, and he thought, okay, so I could screw up making sergeant. But that kid's family could be trapped in a burning building – anything. He clicked the radio on. 'Two-Zero Alpha this is Two-One Bravo. Request permission to suspend exercise. Over.'

'This had better be good, Eddie,' Paddy muttered as he and his section scrambled up the chalky hillside after the boy. The child was much nimbler than they were, and he was way ahead of them. Every so often he would pause to turn back and peer anxiously at them, or gabble something desperately in Greek.

They crested the hill and started down the other side. Eddie ran on ahead, closing the gap between him and the boy. Suddenly he came to a dead halt. 'Corporal!' he yelled. He caught the lad by the hand to stop him running any further.

Paddy caught up with him, with the rest of the section a little way behind. A tarmac road cut across the grassy flank of the hill, which dropped away steeply on the other side. But what held Paddy's attention was the little blue car that had pinwheeled off the road and now lay on its side right on the edge of the drop-off. A truck was skewed across the scrub at the roadside. A man's body lay nearby, arms and legs splayed at unnatural angles.

'Oh shit,' Paddy muttered. 'Dave, check him out –' he pointed to the truck. Dave trotted off, all his larki-ness forgotten now there was a real problem. 'Eddie, have a look in the car.'

Eddie let go of the lad's hand and ran across the road. The boy made to follow him. Paddy grabbed the back of his shirt, and when he still didn't stop, swung him around and picked him up. 'No you stay here with me, mate,' he said.

'Mamma, mamma,' the boy whimpered. It was the most understandable thing he'd said so far.

'Andy,' Paddy said. 'Hold on to him.' He handed the boy over to an uncomfortable looking Fusilier Knox. 'Get your weapons off, lads,' Paddy finished.

After that all he could do was watch as Eddie approached the car. He went round one side then came back and crept gingerly to the other side. Mean-while, Dave tended to the man.

'What have you got, Eddie?' Paddy shouted when he couldn't bear it any longer.

'One casualty. A woman.' Christ, Paddy thought. For the first time he was glad the boy couldn't speak English. 'She's alive,' Eddie finished.

Thank God, Paddy thought.

He radioed in.

Paddy thought that when Major Voce and the other officers arrived, everything would be all right. He was wrong. Acting under orders from Lieutenant Forsythe, he got Knox to check out the door. Reporting back he was just in time to hear Major Voce say to the Lieutenant, 'Okay – if the chopper's out of the question, find out how long an ambulance will take.' He acknowledged Paddy's presence, but turned first to speak to Major McCudden, the doctor, and said, 'We ought to get her out of here quickly – the car looks pretty unstable. Can we move her?'

'As far as I can tell.' The doctor glanced towards the car. Eddie was standing next to it, looking desperately worried. 'But you're right about being quick,' the doctor continued. 'She's lost a lot of blood, and she's got quite bad leg injuries as well.'

Finally, Voce turned to Paddy. 'Corporal?'

'The door won't shift, Sir,' he said. 'It's jammed up against the main frame.'

McCudden sighed heavily. 'Well, there's not much I can do till you get her out. I'll go and have a look at the other driver.' He moved off to where Dave was still applying first aid to the injured man.

Voce looked thoughtful for a moment. Then he said, 'Right. Sarn't Major Stubbs, get a team down there and stabilize the car. Colour Sarn't Ryan get the road closed.'

From the calm way he said it you'd think he was

42

directing an exercise rather than trying to save a woman's life. Paddy had seen him be just as calm under fire in Bosnia, and he thought the same now as he had then – how the hell do you learn to make decisions that easily? He'd often wondered if the major felt that gut-churning moment of terror when he had a hard choice to make.

He supposed you learned it a little at a time – when he looked at the state Lieutenant Forsythe got in, he was sure of it. Yet he wasn't convinced that he'd ever get it. But he'd have to if he were going to make sergeant.

As the men erupted into a flurry of activity, McCudden turned back. 'Just a second,' he called out. 'Someone should be with her.'

'I will, Sir,' Eddie said. Paddy and the Major turned to look at him. Major Voce stared at him, assessing, for a second. Paddy knew what he was thinking – that Eddie had cocked up everything that could be cocked up that morning, and was hardly the first choice for a tricky task.

'I'd like to, Sir,' Eddie said. There was an edge to his voice – something more, Paddy thought, than the simple desire to prove he could do a job right. Major Voce glanced at Paddy. Paddy nodded his head almost imperceptibly. Got to give a man a chance, he thought. Besides, he deserved it – if he hadn't faced Ryan down, they might not be here to help the woman at all.

But before Eddie could have his moment of glory, they had to get a line on the car. Paddy, as one of the heftiest men there, went and held on to the back of it while others tied ropes to its underframe and attached them to the rear of one of the trucks. The army vehicle was much heavier than the civilian one. Now all they could do was hope the car frame wouldn't shear off under the strain. The truck rolled slowly forward, and stopped when the lines went taut.

Paddy kept his grip on the car. Couldn't hurt, after all. Eddie and CSM Stubbs were round at the side of the car. 'Right, Sir,' he said. 'All set.'

'Remember, lad – keep her conscious. Reassure her,' the CSM said.

'I'll do my best, Sergeant Major,' Eddie said. Paddy felt the car lurch as Eddie climbed on to it and in through the space where the rear windscreen had been before it had got blown out.

Paddy could hear the murmur of Eddie's voice as he talked to the woman, but not what he said. When she replied, she seemed to be speaking English. That would make things easier. It wasn't a job Paddy would have relished.

'Corporal,' CSM Stubbs said. 'Get a couple of men and lever the door open – quick as you can, we need that woman out of there.'

'Yes, Sir,' Paddy said.

He went and got a tyre iron from the truck, and told Knox to come and give him a hand. 'Steady the car for me,' he said.

'Yes Corp,' Knox said.

Paddy clambered on to the car, which rocked

alarmingly. The woman yelped in pain. 'I said steady it!' he said sharply over his shoulder to Knox.

'Go easy, lads,' Eddie said. He was in the back seat, but he'd reached over to grasp the woman's hand in his much larger one. She was all cut up from flying glass, and her legs had got twisted and wedged under the steering column. Her face was sheened with sweat and her skin was ashen.

Paddy shifted round and managed to slip the tyre iron between the door and its frame. The car lurched, and the woman moaned again.

'Sorry,' Paddy said. 'Just getting my footing.'

'Yeah, well go easy,' Eddie repeated. Paddy hauled on the tyre iron, trying to use as little force as he could, so as to keep the car still while getting the door open. He heard Eddie say, 'Just the lads putting the fear of God up me – ' Paddy caught his eye.

'I so scared,' the woman said in heavily accented English. 'What if something happen to me – what if I die? Who will look after my Panos then?'

Gawd, Paddy thought. Don't think about her, he told himself firmly. Let Eddie do his bit while you concentrate on yours and get this bloody door open.

'Hey,' he heard Eddie say softly, 'no-one's going to die today. After all, you've got the British army on your side.'

Paddy shifted the tyre iron to a new point and heaved. The door gave a little.

'Garvey?' Forsythe asked.

'Almost, Sir,' Paddy said.

'Carry on,' the lieutenant said. Paddy watched him

go out of the corner of his eye. The young officer went over to Major McCudden and spoke to him.

The doctor leaned into the car. 'Nelson, be ready to shift yourself double-quick when I say.'

'Sir,' Eddie called out.

'Come on, you bugger,' Paddy muttered at the door. He wiped his face with the back of his hand to get rid of the sweat, then put all his weight on the tyre iron. Metal screeched and tore, and the door popped open.

The woman started to scream – whether in fright or terror Paddy couldn't say. She clutched convulsively at Eddie. He said, 'For Christ's sake get a move on – she can't take much more of this.'

'Take it easy,' Paddy said. He pulled the woman round towards him, trying to be gentle, but there was no way to be gentle enough. Her screams were hoarse and continuous, and he could see now that her legs had been shattered. White bone poked through the skin beneath her knee, and there was a deep gash, black with congealing blood, on her other thigh.

He glanced back. There were several men waiting to lift her out. 'Eddie,' he said. 'See if you can move forward and get her legs straight.'

Eddie clambered halfway over the front seat. The car bounced ominously. He managed – just – to pull the woman's legs into line with the new orientation of her upper body. Her screams went up half an octave. 'Easy Athina,' he said. 'Not long now. Not long.'

Athina, Paddy thought. She has a name and a kid ... for a second he flashed on the street in Bosnia

46

where he'd done a madman's dash to pull a young girl and her baby out of the line of sniper fire. Then the moment was past, and he was back in the dust and heat of Cyprus instead of on the dusty streets of Sarajevo.

'Lift on a count of three,' Major Voce said. He counted them down, and suddenly they were lifting Athina out of the car head first.

'Nelson – move,' Major McCudden said.

As Paddy helped the other men lay the woman down on an emergency stretcher, he saw Eddie scramble out of the back of the car.

'It's going!' someone yelled.

The car started to roll slowly forwards. The metal the rope was tied to bent slowly. Paddy stood up and took a pace or two towards the car. There was a thunderous crack and something – rope or metal – gave up the struggle. The car hurtled forward. It paused for a long moment, suspended on the point of the rock like a weighing scale. Then it toppled over, turned once in mid-air, and was gone.

Paddy rushed to the edge in time to see it bounce once, twice and a third time at the bottom of the slope. The air was suddenly thick with the stink of petrol. There was a dull whump and the car erupted into a ball of orange flame. A plume of greasy black smoke billowed up from it. Even at that distance, the heat of it was enough to bring a flush to Paddy's face. A moment later the fire spread to the surrounding scrub, where it smouldered and crackled.

'Mamma?' said a childish voice from behind Paddy.

Paddy turned. The little lad – Panos, wasn't that what Athina had called him – was standing there, forgotten by just about everyone.

'Your Mum's going to be just fine,' he said. 'Just fine.'

He hoped it was true.

Paddy stood at ease in the cool shadow cast by Major Voce's office. He and Eddie had been told to report to the Major, and Paddy was pretty sure it was about their poor performance in the exercise that morning. Bollocking time, in other words.

Dave wandered past, making a mock inspection. He looked them up and down, knowing they couldn't react. 'I reckon you'll get a medal,' he said at last to Eddie. 'Like Paddy. He was ever such a hero in –'

'Piss off, Dave,' Paddy cut in.

Lieutenant Forsythe appeared at one end of the building. 'Tucker!' All three men snapped to attention. 'Phone call. I hope it's an emergency, Tucker.'

'Sir!' Dave started slowly towards the company office.

Shit, Paddy thought. Donna. It had to be – there was no way she'd come all the way to Cyprus early and not want to see Dave. It was going to lead to trouble. He could feel it in his gut. Yet part of him envied Dave – and then he realized with a start that he'd barely thought about Nancy since that morning.

He hadn't had time to consider that properly before CSM Stubbs came out and called them in. They stood to attention, then marched in. Eddie looked terrified.

'Here we go,' Paddy whispered to him, trying to sound more confident than he felt.

Once inside it was immediately obvious that the Major wasn't about to pin any medals on them. He wasn't that much older than Paddy – five years or so, yet he had the sternness and authority of a much older man. Major McCudden lounged on a table near the back wall of the office.

Eddie and Paddy saluted and were announced by Stubbs, then stood at attention.

'Well, your performance in the Fibua was a complete and utter shambles,' Major Voce said. Paddy had to struggle to meet his gaze. 'Any explanation?' He was looking directly at Paddy, who could find nothing to say that wouldn't land Eddie in it.

Then Eddie said, 'It was my fault, Sir. I overdid things last night.'

'Thank you,' the Major said quietly. His quietness was worse than any tongue-lashing he could have given them. But it wasn't over yet. 'So tell me, Corporal Garvey.' Here it comes, Paddy thought. 'What were you doing when it was all getting out of hand? Exercising your authority?'

The awful thing was that he made it a straightforward question. Sarcasm would have been easier to take. Paddy groped for an answer. 'Not enough, Sir,' he said at last.

'No. That was clear,' Major Voce said. He stared at them for a long moment, in which Paddy had enough time to decide he'd better get used to the idea of losing at least one of his stripes. But then the Major went on, 'Under normal circumstances I'd have no qualms about putting you both on the next plane back to Germany. However –' he paused, letting them squirm for a bit longer, ' – you did well at the crash today, so I'm letting it go.' Relief swamped Paddy, so that he could barely stammer a thank you. The major wasn't through with them, though. 'But,' he continued, and now there was a real snap in his voice, 'I want to see a marked improvement across the rest of Lion Sun. If not, I'm going to come down on you very, very hard. Is that clear?'

'Sir!' Paddy and Eddie said together.

'March 'em out, Sar'nt-Major,' Major Voce said.

Before CSM Stubbs could give the order, Eddie said, 'Permission to speak, Sir.' Sergeant Major Stubbs came forward and flicked him on the shoulder, hard enough to get his attention without really hurting. 'I'd like to see Athina, Sir,' Eddie said without waiting for permission to be granted. 'The woman in the hospital, Sir,' he stumbled on.

Major Voce glared at him. 'Nelson, you're on a military exercise, not a social workers' course.'

'I know, Sir,' Eddie said. You had to admire him for his sheer pigheadedness if nothing else, Paddy thought. Once he got started there was just no stopping him. 'I'd just like to see her.'

Major Voce stared at him for a long moment, as if he couldn't believe what he was hearing. 'Straight there, straight back,' he said in the end. 'Two hours, that's all.'

'Thank you, Sir,' Eddie said.

The major's expression suggested that he didn't quite believe what he'd just said. 'Sar'nt!' he said.

CSM Stubbs marched them out. When they were well clear of the office, Paddy said, 'You'll chance your arm one time too many, sunshine.'

'Yeah, well,' Eddie said. 'I just want to make sure she's okay – she hasn't got anyone to help her, you know. The lad's father was a tourist and he doesn't even know about the kid. And her family threw her out –'

'Don't get involved,' Paddy said; he suddenly remembered Midnight Rawlings, and how he'd fallen for a prostitute in Hong Kong; he'd almost chucked his career in for her.

'Nah,' Eddie said. 'But I've got a present for the kid.' He pulled a battered old mouth organ out of his pocket. 'My mum used to say this was my dad's – that he left it when he bogged off back to Jamaica.'

'Oh yeah?' Paddy said.

'Me, I think she picked it up at a jumble sale –' Eddie's tone said he thought no such thing. 'Anyway, I thought the kid might like it.'

'Probably drive his mum nuts with it,' Paddy conceded. 'Anyway, you'd better get going – they probably started counting your two hours from the second you left the office.'

'Take it easy,' Eddie said. He headed off in the direction of the main gate. Before he got very far he stopped and turned back. 'Paddy? I'm sorry about this morning.'

'Don't worry about it, mate,' Paddy said. 'I'm sorry

about last night, if it comes to it.' And then, feeling much more cheerful, he went to grab a shower.

Paddy came out of the barracks, stripped to the waist with his towel over one shoulder and his soap bag in the other hand. Tomorrow, he thought, I'll do better. I'll figure out a way to get through to that pillock Dave that he has to behave – he was lucky he wasn't up in front of Voce with me and Eddie – and I'll show 'em what I can do.

Dave chose that moment to appear at his side. 'That was Donna on the phone,' he said.

As if I hadn't guessed, Paddy thought. 'Keep your voice down, mate,' Paddy answered.

'She wants to see me tonight,' Dave went on, like he was a schoolboy, discussing a date. 'Paphos. You in?'

I might have known it. I *did* know it Paddy thought. 'No, Dave,' he said firmly. 'I am not going into Paphos.' Not now he'd suddenly turned into Major Voce's special project for the duration of Operation Lion Sun.

'We are talking about the woman I love,' Dave said.

Paddy laughed shortly. 'I'm sorry, mate,' he said. He'd spent the best part of yesterday moping around over whether he should have given up his career for his wife – now Dave wanted him to chuck it in for Donna. 'I'm going to clean up,' he said, gesturing at the shower block with his soap bag. 'Then I'm going to the Naafi for something to eat, and I'm going to get

52

my head down.' He was suddenly angry with Dave for even suggesting they do something that would land them in it again. 'If you had any sense, you'd do the same.'

Of course, expecting Dave to have sense was like asking a fish to ride a bicycle. 'I haven't got any choice, have I?' he demanded.

'What are you talking about?' Paddy asked, knowing he didn't want to hear the answer.

'Some Cypriot bloke's after her.' Paddy stopped walking and turned to face his friend. 'I don't think he's after idle chat and a plate of tzatziki,' Dave said. It wouldn't be the first time Donna'd played away.

Paddy sighed. 'All right, mate,' he said at last.

Dave and Paddy shared the bus to Paphos with ten other people, three crates of chickens and a sack of rapidly fermenting oranges. Since the bus appeared to have lost any remnants of its suspension ten years previously, by the time Paddy clambered out he felt as if he'd gone ten rounds in the ring with the company boxing champion.

Dave had got out of the bus just ahead of him. Paddy caught up with him and they stood in the middle of the dusty square for a moment, squinting at the low ochre buildings that surrounded it. One of them had a tacky blue sign over the door proclaiming it to be a taverna.

What the bloody hell am I doing here when Voce has threatened to take me apart if I misbehave? Paddy wondered. Following Dave Tucker to my doom, that's what.

'You and me are through, Dave,' he said, only half-joking. He put his hands on his hips.

Dave licked his lips. 'Really?'

'Yeah. We've outgrown each other.' It wasn't so far off the truth.

Dave craned round and stared deep into Paddy's eyes. 'But we were good together, weren't we, Paddy?'

Paddy slapped him lightly on the shoulder. 'The best.' He stripped off his jacket and Dave did the same. 'Right. Prepare for hostilities.' They headed for the taverna. 'I never really wanted to be a sergeant anyway,' he said.

Inside, the taverna was cool and dark. Traditional music blared out from the local band playing in the corner. Marcia Stubbs and Donna were sitting at one of the tables, with a younger woman who could only be Donna's kid sister Kelly. If there was local opposition, it was making itself scarce in the face of the British army.

Dave sat down next to Donna. He didn't look pleased. Under the circumstances, Paddy decided that discretion was the better part of valour and found himself a seat next to Marcia. Pretty soon he was deep into the meal, and Marcia was regaling him with a story about how a local taxi driver had tried to overcharge them and Donna had refused to pay. The food came – spicy mincemeat wrapped in fig leaves, and then lamb with rice. And glass after glass of retsina.

This, Paddy thought eyeing his glass, is a bad idea. Then he picked it up and drained it.

A couple of people from another table got up to dance. Paddy felt a tug on his arm – Marcia, wanting to dance. He followed her on to the floor, and they linked arms. A local girl took his other side and started to teach them the dance. Donna and Dave joined them, and for a while it was good fun.

But of local lotharios there were none in sight. Conned again, Paddy thought, but he didn't mind, and knew it was the drink making him mellow.

Dave said something to Donna. The wrong thing. She flounced off to the bar. He followed her.

Here we go, Paddy thought. Yet another Dave and Donna special. Their rows were legendary – the only thing he was sure of was that in a couple of days they'd be all over each other again. He reached out and linked up with the woman on his far side to complete the chain.

Suddenly Donna shouted, 'I want something of me very own, Dave – nothing to do with the sodding army.'

'Yeah,' Dave yelled back. 'Well like it or not I'm in the army, Donna – that's just the way it is – '

Donna got up and stalked out. Dave stared at her retreating back. He took a couple of steps towards her. Paddy hurried over and grabbed him. 'Don't do it, mate,' he said. 'You know what she's like – leave her alone to get on with it and by the time local leave comes round she'll have forgotten all about it.'

'Yeah,' Dave said. He scowled, went back to the bar and called for another bottle of retsina.

The fence around Bloodhound Camp was tall. Very,

very tall. But nothing a couple of fit squaddies couldn't handle. Paddy scrambled to the top, hung there for a second, then dropped heavily down inside.

Dave was just a split second behind him, but had obviously decided to go for the soft option because he landed heavily on Paddy.

Paddy yelped, then realized they were making too much noise. He turned to Dave and put his fingers to his lips. 'Shhh!' he said, loud enough to make sure Dave heard him.

They sneaked across the grounds to the barracks. The whole place was in darkness. Paddy eased the door open and they slid inside. They tiptoed with difficulty across the cramped room.

Dave crashed into a bucket and mop. 'Shh,' he said to the room in general.

We're done for, Paddy thought. But the day's activities must have taken it all out of everyone, because no-one woke up. He slid, fully clothed into bed. So did Dave.

For a moment there was quiet. Then Dave's bed erupted into a flurry of sheets and blankets. He leapt out, grabbed a squash racket and started thrashing his bed with it. 'Snake,' he screamed. 'Snake!'

Paddy flicked the lights on and got out of bed – and just at that moment everyone else in the barracks burst out laughing. Dave pulled the bedclothes back and looked at something long and green in his bed.

It didn't move.

Dave stared at it in disgust, and then at Eddie, who was lying back in his bed laughing his head off.

Dave picked the thing up, and Paddy realized it was a length of stripped willow. Eddie hissed at Dave. Dave turned to Paddy. 'Yes. But would it make my Donna a nice handbag?'

# Chapter 3

If anyone had told Paddy that swimming in the sea off Cyprus could seem like a bad idea, he wouldn't have believed them.

Mind you, he wouldn't normally have been contemplating doing it in full combat uniform – boots and all – with Colour Sergeant Ryan screaming insults at him.

The big marine stood in front of Two Platoon. 'Right,' he shouted, loud enough that they could have heard him in Paphos. 'One fighting man with a stretch of water to traverse. One pair of boots. A helmet. A weapon. And a bergen. End result – a flotation pack.' His flat voice turned the words into bullets. He jabbed his finger towards a large green object on the ground. 'Here is one I prepared earlier.' Ryan dropped to a prone position behind the flotation pack, and with one smooth movement brought his weapon round to bear, using the pack as a rest for his arms.

'Welcome back "Blue Peter", all is forgiven,' Paddy whispered to Eddie. As far as he was concerned, the only good thing about this was that it marked the beginning of the end of Operation Lion Sun. He'd really been looking forward to it, but Ryan had made near enough the whole six weeks a misery. Still, there was just this and the beach-landing exercise to go, and then it was back to Muenster.

Even Tony was having trouble suppressing a grin. 'This is what happens when you bring the Marines in,' he muttered.

'I thought he was going to teach us survival training?' Eddie asked no-one in particular.

'Wombat catching tomorrow,' Dave said. 'Day after that, how to put out forest fires with snot and a packet of teacakes.'

Ryan glared up at them from his position on the sand. 'I'll pretend I didn't hear that, Fusilier,' he said. He climbed to his feet. 'Now, pay attention because I'm going to show you this once and once only.' He grabbed the pack in front of Eddie, and with a few deft twists and yanks, plus a good few lungfuls of air, turned it into a flotation pack. Eddie grinned.

'Don't get excited, Fusilier,' Ryan said. He pulled the pack apart until it was once again the bergen it had started as. 'You still get to make one of your very own – that goes for all of you.'

They tried. Paddy had made less of a mess as a lad with a model aeroplane kit. Eventually, they all had something resembling a flotation pack.

'Right,' Ryan yelled. 'You've had enough time. Let's get wet.' The men stared at him. 'Move it!' he roared. 'Last one in goes twice round the rock.'

Paddy grabbed his pack and ran. The rock was a good half mile away, and in this heat he could well do without an extra cross-country run.

The disasters started once they got into the water. They waded out with the packs in front of them.

'Come on, come on – no prizes for keeping your hair dry, you girlies,' Ryan yelled from the beach.

'What is this? Escape from Devil's Island?' Paddy asked. He thought he was doing all right – he'd even managed to get his rifle on top of the pack, where it wasn't quite getting soaked with water. 'These are only supposed to be used for river crossings.' To prove his point, a wavelet sloshed over him and made him gasp.

'Welcome to the wet wet world of Colour Sergeant Ryan,' Tony said from behind him. It was all right for him – he didn't have a pack to deal with.

Dave turned to say something, but it made him lose his grip on the pack. 'Oops,' he said. 'It's gone tits up.' The pack turned over in the water. There was a horrible glugging noise and it sank slowly out of sight.

'Dive for your gear, Fusilier,' Ryan bellowed. When Dave hesitated, he yelled again, 'Dive for it!'

'Better do it, Dave,' Tony said, and then, 'Hang on – what's this? The cavalry's coming over the hill.'

Paddy turned round, keeping a careful grip on his own pack. CSM Stubbs was walking down the beach, scowling furiously.

'Aye well, it's too late for me,' Dave said. He struck a tragic pose. 'Tell Donna I love her, and tell her to give Macaulay my medals when he reaches eighteen.' Then he kicked his legs up and disappeared beneath the surface.

'Trouble on shore,' Eddie said.

He was right. CSM Stubbs was talking to Ryan, and whatever he was saying, the Marine didn't like it. In fact, both men looked furious.

Suddenly, the sergeant major strode up to the water's edge. 'Sarn't Wilton,' he bellowed. Tony acknowledged him. 'Get these men out. Now!'

'Come on, my lovelies,' Tony said. 'Paddling time's over.'

They struggled towards the shore. CSM Stubbs was already leaving. Ryan glared at them. His face was fixed like granite. Only the slow jumping of a muscle in his jaw revealed his rage.

The beach-landing exercise was to take place in two days' time. The men were given passes to go out that night, since they'd have the day in between off, and Paddy was determined to enjoy himself. Donna and Dave were arguing intensely. Paddy just couldn't be bothered to get involved, but he gathered it was about Donna's kid sister Kelly — she'd fallen for some local lad, gone off with him that morning and hadn't been seen since.

Paddy grabbed himself a beer, then looked around to see what was what. The place was full of a new batch of tourists — you could tell them by their pale skins. A slim, dark-haired woman with a bright smile caught his eye.

'Go on then,' Eddie said. 'You know you want to.'

'After you, mate,' Paddy said.

Before long he was happily bopping on the dance

floor, first with the dark-haired girl and then with one with strawberry blonde hair. After a bit, Tony and Marsha Stubbs joined them. You'd never have thought Marsha was the CSM's wife the way she was carrying on. As for Tony he was clutching a can in one hand and a bit of paper in the other. Paddy recognized it – Tony had been showing it around earlier: it was a scan of the new baby, which wasn't due for quite a while.

'Here we go,' Marsha called out. She grabbed Tony by the hand and swung him in close. He slid down on to the floor and rolled easily to his knees, playing the air guitar while something with a heavy seventies beat blared out of the sound system. Paddy and a few of the others started to clap in time to the music. One of the girls Paddy had danced with earlier came up and stood next to him. She started clapping along. He caught her eye and she gave him a tiny smile, somewhere between shy and flirtatious.

Going to be a good night tonight, Paddy me boy, he thought to himself.

Suddenly, Donna appeared in front of Paddy. 'Have you got a condom, Paddy?' she yelled, leaving him hoping that the music wouldn't suddenly fade.

'You're unreal, you are, Donna,' Paddy said. What the bloody hell was she playing at, with Dave not three feet away?

She moved in so close it should have been illegal in a public place. 'Oh hey – they're not for me, they're for Kelly.' She groped him. He yelped 'What are you doing?' before he realized she'd shoved her hand in the front pocket of his jeans.

He glanced over at the girl. She was staring at him in fascination – the way a rabbit might look at a weasel, say.

'Aha!' Donna exclaimed triumphantly. She held up the packet of three condoms he'd been saving for a lucky day. 'Look,' she said. Paddy followed her gaze. Kelly was near the bar, wrapped around a young Cypriot guy. 'She's got a clean bill of health and no kids,' Donna said. 'I want her to stay that way.'

Paddy hissed in her ear, 'What about me? I might get lucky here – '

'Get through three of these and you're not the only one who's getting lucky,' Donna said. She pulled one of the condoms out of the pack. 'One for Kelly, one for you.' She jammed the single condom in the breast pocket of his shirt. Then she glanced at the girl, grinned and stuck the third one in with it. 'If you think you're up to it . . .' she said, and moved away.

She might as well have taken the lot. By the time Paddy had turned round, the girl had gone.

It was just as well they had the next day off. When Paddy woke up he had a head like a lead balloon and his mouth felt like something small and furry had died in it. And he was alone, as he had been all night. He swung his legs over the edge of the bed and contemplated standing up. Bad idea, he decided. Mind you, if he didn't get up soon he'd miss breakfast at the Naafi. Then he realized that was an even worse idea anyway.

'Get you a glass of water, Corp?' Eddie said. It was all right for him – he'd been on orange juice all night.

'Ha ha very funny,' Paddy said. Then he thought about it a bit more. 'Yeah. All right.'

Eddie wandered off and came back with a glass. 'You hear about Donna's sister?' he asked.

'No,' Paddy said wearily. He wasn't sure he wanted to know. If it hadn't been for Kelly, he might have had a better time. 'What about her?'

'She's getting married to that bloke she was with. Donna's in a real tizz and Dave's all over the place about it.'

Paddy gulped the water down. It didn't help. The way he felt, nothing was going to help unless it involved transplanting his entire body. 'Tell you what,' he said. 'You help Dave sort it out, then come and tell me all about it and I'll recommend you for a medal.' He collapsed sideways on the bed, shut his eyes and refused to think about anything except how disgusting he felt.


The human body was an amazing thing, Paddy decided. For instance, by the time for the beach-landing exercise rolled around the next day, he actually felt quite human again.

He stood with the rest of the men on the beach. It was a sweltering hot day, and not even the cool sea breeze could stop the sweat trickling down his back and soaking through his combat jacket. To make things worse, they were already wearing their life-jackets.

Tony paced up and down in front of them, clutching a clipboard which he glanced at from time to time. 'Right,' he said, shouting over the noise of the engines of the three Rigid Raider craft that were waiting for them out in the bay. 'I want everyone fully cammed up. I want everyone with their lifejackets fully secured. Belt order on top unbuckled, weapons loosely secured to the sides of the craft.' He paused and came to a halt front and centre. 'Do not – do *not* – remove your lifejackets, under any circumstances, unless instructed to do so.' He glanced over to Ryan, who was standing next to Lieutenant Forsythe. 'And for the non-sailors among you, your favourite marine colour sergeant is on the rescue boat. Any of you wishing to reacquaint yourselves with the contents of your alimentary canals had better do so over the sides of the boat and quietly. I thank you.' He stared at them. Forsythe told him to carry on. 'Right,' he said. 'Mount up.'

The three Rigid Raiders roared toward the shore in a fountain of spray, each one piloted by a Royal Marine. There was a fourth craft, but it was the rescue boat. Ryan went towards that, while the platoon divided itself up among the others. Paddy, Dave and Nelson splashed through the surf towards one of the boats.

'Got the sea in me veins, me,' Dave said as he struggled aboard the craft.

'Oh yeah?' Paddy asked, knowing he was going to regret it.

'Me Grandad ran pedaloes out of Whitley Bay,' Dave said. The boats sped out to sea, and before long

65

he was miming paddling a canoe and singing something that he probably thought sounded like a Maori chant.

'Give over, Dave,' Eddie said.

Dave looked properly hurt, and only shut up when the Marine pilot turned round and scowled at him. A little while later, he'd gone a peculiar puce colour, and a little while later he followed Tony's instructions and let his lunch go over the side of the boat.

'Grub's up for the fishes, then?' Paddy asked.

'Oh God, just let me die here,' Dave moaned.

'Oh come on, Dave,' Paddy replied. 'You know what they say about sea-sickness – it won't kill you. It'll just make you wish you were dead.'

Two Platoon were in the second attack wave. They waited off-shore while Phase One went ahead. In the distance, gunfire rattled across the bay and plumes of yellow and red smoke billowed up providing cover for the attackers. Paddy scanned the headland, knowing that Major Voce and Colonel Jennings were up there somewhere, directing both the attack and the defence. He was suddenly up for it – he wanted to get on the ground, feel the weight of the SA80 in his hands and feel it buck as he let fly. Come on, he thought at them. Let us go.

A movement in his peripheral vision attracted his attention. He turned to see Dave taking off his life-jacket. Stupid bastard, he thought, glaring at him. 'Dave, man – what you playing at?'

'I'm not wearing that,' Dave said. 'Smells like Macaulay's underpants.' He still looked really ill.

Yeah, and we know who'll get done for it if you're caught – me as well as you, for not exercising my authority. But he knew that look of Dave's – that bolshie, defiant-brat look that it would cost more grief than it was worth to bully his way through. 'Suit yourself,' Paddy said, as disgusted with himself for not being prepared to argue as he was with Dave.

Besides, the sea was as flat as a millpond, even if Dave didn't think so –

And at that moment all three Marine pilots opened their throttles and raced for the beach. The engines howled. The bow of the Raider lifted up as it picked up speed. The craft literally skipped across the sea, bouncing from wave to wave. Dave yelped and flailed around. Paddy grabbed the side of the boat.

For a minute it was okay. Then Paddy spotted something brightly coloured in the water. He heard Tony shout a warning. The Raider banked and he felt himself slide. He grabbed on, but saw Dave crash into Eddie and then both go spinning off into the air.

'Dave! Eddie!' Tony screamed.

The Raider righted itself. Eddie was treading water nearby, and for a second so was Dave. Then he slipped beneath the surface.

'Where the hell is Dave?' Paddy muttered; but even as he spoke he was tearing off his helmet and life-jacket. The Raider circled back to where they'd lost the men.

Paddy scrambled to the prow and dived off before anyone could stop him. He knifed through the water towards the only hope he had – Dave's lifejacket bobbing around on the surface – dimly aware that the rescue boat had arrived and that Ryan was doing the same thing. He heard Tony yelling at Eddie to stay where he was.

He took a deep breath and dived. He could barely see three feet through the water. Down, he thought. Further down. He pushed on, until his chest hurt and his throat burned, but there was nothing there. He scythed upwards, and even as his head broke the surface he was screaming Dave's name.

'Go under, Paddy,' Tony shouted. 'Go on!'

Colour Sergeant Ryan came up for air just as Paddy went down again. Be here, mate, Paddy thought. Be there for Paddy 'cause I ain't coming up without you.

Something moved, greyish in the murky water. He could barely breathe but that didn't matter. He swam over to it. His hand grabbed at it – got a handful of material. Then he was on his way up.

'I've got him,' he sobbed. 'I've got him.' Ryan swam over to him. 'Here, take him off me,' Paddy said. Suddenly there was no strength in his arms and legs, and he had a terrible thought – what if Dave were dead. What would he say to Donna? But he couldn't think of that. He doggy-paddled over to the rescue boat, the best he could do, and did his best to help Tony haul first Dave and then Ryan out of the water.

He grabbed on to the side of the boat, but there was a sudden swell and he drifted under its upthrust prow. Another sudden surge drove him upwards. He felt his head hit the boat, and a split second later a tremendous pain lanced across his skull and right down his neck. He grunted in surprise and lost his grip on the boat.

He felt himself drift backwards, but it didn't really bother him, even though he suddenly realized he wasn't wearing his lifejacket. Eddie was shouting something at him, but it was hardly important. 'I've hit my head,' he said after a bit to shut him up.

A wave rolled over him, filling his mouth and nose with water. Gonna do a Tucker, he thought. Going under. But then someone grabbed him. 'You're knackered,' Eddie's voice said, out of a greenish haze that was all Paddy could see.

I can see the sea, he thought, but that's all I can see. 'Where's Dave?' he asked. Got to concentrate, he thought, but he felt half asleep.

'He's all right,' Eddie said. 'He's safe.'

'Good,' Paddy said. 'Wouldn't want to get on Donna's bad side – ' He felt himself being shoved along in the water, and then he was being lifted up. Something hard slammed into his belly, and then it felt like his arms were being torn out of their sockets.

There was a hell of a lot of noise. Someone said, 'He hasn't got a pulse – '

Dave! Paddy thought. He struggled to sit up, but someone's arms restrained him. He realized he was out of the water. Out of the sea. So he should be able to see something, not just the horrible greenish murk – only it wasn't green any more, just a kind of colourless nothing.

'Something's wrong,' he said.

Somewhere, someone was praying. Ryan, he thought. That's Ryan's voice: 'Remember, O most loving Virgin Mary, it is a thing unheard of –' and then he lost it in a confusion of grunts and shouts and the roar of the engine.

He had to see, but he couldn't see. He struggled against Eddie. 'Something's not right here,' he said, fighting down the hysteria that threatened to overwhelm him.

'You've taken a knock, that's all,' Eddie said.

'I can't see a bloody thing,' he moaned, appalled at how close to tears he sounded.

'Beautiful,' Tony's voice said, cutting through all the other sounds. 'Beautiful, Dave – I thought for a minute I was going to have to tell Donna you'd caught it.'

'Dave!' Paddy called out.

'Take it easy, Paddy,' Eddie said. 'He's all right, now. Everything's going to be all right.'

Paddy lay back. He shut his eyes. At least that way it was normal not to be able to see. He took a long, wavering breath. The boat bucked and roared beneath him, and a faint smell of petrol cut the ozone tang of the breeze. They'll get me out of this soon, he thought. Get the doc and he'll fix me up. He had to think that. Anything else was too scary.

The sound of the engine died and the Raider coasted to a halt. There was a babble of voices – Greek and English with varying accents, and a woman's voice, loud and imperious.

'Where the bloody hell are we?' he asked, wondering if there were anyone nearby to hear the question.

70

'Tourist beach,' Eddie said. 'Up you get now.' Paddy felt hands on his arms. He struggled to get his feet under him, but bizarrely even without being able to see he could feel the world spinning. He put his arm round Eddie's shoulder and allowed himself to be guided forward, and obediently raised his feet to step over the side of the boat. His combat uniform hung in sodden folds against his body, and he kept wanting to laugh. He couldn't even see the sea, now.

There was someone else there now. He let whoever it was take part of his weight, and staggered up the beach between Eddie and the new person.

They made him stand with his back towards something hard. Belatedly he identified the thing sticking into his back as – probably – the handle of a car door.

'Take it very, very easy,' said Major McCudden's soft Scottish burr.

'Doc?' Paddy muttered.

'He was complaining about his sight,' Eddie said.

Paddy felt a hand on his face, gently steadying his head. He felt the panic welling up in him again. 'I can't see, Doc,' he said. He felt the hands touch his forehead and eyelids. 'I can't bloody see,' he repeated. He was appalled to feel tears running down his face.

'Okay, Garvey. You stay absolutely still. Don't move a muscle.'

'What's the story?' The voice was older. A man's. Colonel Jennings, Paddy eventually identified it as. If he's here, I'm a goner, Paddy thought.

'Closed wound to the back of the head,' the doctor answered.

'Bad news?' That was Jennings again.

I might as well not be here, Paddy thought. It was easier to get angry about that than to look into the greyness that was all he could see.

'Like the boy said,' McCudden replied. 'He's gone blind.'

# Chapter 4

Paddy moved smoothly through the darkness. He was in a wheelchair pushed by a nurse, and he was terrified. His hands clutched damply at the leatherette arms of the chair. The hospital smock they had helped him change into clung sweatily to his body. He strained to see into the darkness, but there was nothing there. If he could see anything – a shadow, a flash of light, anything at all – maybe he wouldn't have to go through with the scan they wanted him to have.

He could hear the padding of the nurse's rubber-soled shoes on the vinyl, and McCudden's heavier tread. There were voices in the distance, and some-where a telephone shrilled.

Paddy's feet touched something which moved away; then moving air brushed his cheeks and he realized they'd gone through a pair of swing doors.

The thought of the scanner terrified him. If they found out he had brain damage . . . if this was it for ever and ever, just the darkness and people being kind to him, and groping his way round a world limited to places he knew well . . . if that were it then his life was over. He felt panic shut his throat and threaten to engulf him. His heart hammered and his mouth went dry.

'Doc?' he said, suddenly unsure whether McCudden was still there or not. He was appalled at how frightened he felt.

'I'm here, Garvey.' The man's voice was deep and resonant.

'You must be joking if you think I'm going in that tunnel by myself,' Paddy said. He tried to make it sound funny, but there was a wobble in his voice he hadn't meant to put there.

'It's quite comfortable really,' McCudden said. 'Like having a lie down in a Ferrari, except that the Ferrari's probably cheaper.'

Paddy thought of the tube closing over him, like a coffin, threatening to bear down and smother him. It didn't matter that he wouldn't be able to see it. He'd know. He'd be able to sense the weight of it around him. And if the scan brought back the wrong result, the machine might as well be a coffin. 'Sorry, doc,' he said. He couldn't say any of what he was really thinking. McCudden had already seen him cry once. Paddy would be damned before he'd make it twice. 'I get a bit funny in tunnels. Nurse here'll have to come in with me.'

'I'm afraid there isn't room for two in there, Corporal,' she said. She was laughing, but beneath that her tone was firm.

Suddenly Paddy couldn't do it any more – couldn't keep up the banter when all around him there was darkness. 'Shit,' he said. He clutched convulsively at the arms of the chair. 'I'm scared of what that thing'll show.'

The nurse brought the chair to a halt. 'What it'll show is how we're going to sort you out, isn't it, doctor?' she said with practised compassion. Her voice was very close to his ear, as if she'd bent low to talk to him. He could smell her – soap and starch and just a trace of perfume beneath.

'That is what you want, isn't it, Paddy?' McCudden said softly, as if he were talking to a frightened child.

Paddy could hardly breathe. Sort me out, he thought. Take me out of the darkness. He realized he was shaking. I can't, he thought. I can't do this . . .

Bosnia had been easier. Northern Ireland was. You were with your mates and you cracked a joke and went out and faced the snipers. You blanked off the fear of death with the boring detail of everyday routine. You kept alert and that stopped you thinking about it too much – and if you were down, someone else was up and so it went, all the days until the tour was over.

But this was different. This was just him, and the darkness, and knowing there might be years of it ahead.

A sniper's bullet would have been kinder.

There was nothing to do but get on with it. He drew a long, shuddering breath. 'Yeah,' he said. 'That's what I want.'

'Let's do it, then,' McCudden said.

Waiting for the results was almost worse than having the scan done. Not being able to do anything much only made it worse, and the sedation had left him feeling weak and bilious. All Paddy could do was lie there and think about what had happened. If he thought of one thing he could have done to avoid the accident, he thought of a hundred. For starters he should have made Dave keep his lifejacket on. And he should have been more alert – warned everyone to hang on when he first saw the barrel, rather than depending on them hearing Tony in the rescue boat. Or if not that, he should at least have had the sense to keep clear of the side of the boat till they got Dave aboard . . .

Anything, anything at all. Yet it was too late, like it was too late for him and Nancy, and even Christine had not only met someone else while he was in Bosnia, she'd actually married him. Well, Paddy thought to himself. I guess I can kiss goodbye to a love life now. Unless I want to be a charity date, that is –

The door clicked open.

'Who's there?' Paddy demanded. Christ, he thought – it could be an axe murderer for all I know. It had been a long time since he'd felt so helpless.

'McCudden,' said a soft Scottish voice. The door slammed shut. Footsteps approached the bed. There was a clatter, perhaps of a chair being moved.

Paddy hauled himself up on the pillows. It took all his strength. 'Hiya,' he said.

'I've just been speaking to the neurologist,' McCudden said.

'Oh aye,' Paddy said, but he thought, I don't want

76

to know. I don't want to know, for Christ's sake. But he had to know. 'What did he say?'

'I'm afraid you're going to have to stay with us for a while.'

The words were like hammerblows. Paddy licked his lips. 'Just tell me what's going on, doc.' He paused. Part of him wanted platitudes, to think that he was doing well. But he had to know the worst. 'And please, no bullshit,' he added finally.

'Well, when you banged your head against the side of the boat, you gave yourself a brain haemorrhage around the area of the optical cortex –'

'Right,' Paddy said. He knew what all the words meant, but he couldn't put them together and make them make sense – not with that word haemorrhage in there: he thought of accident victims living out their lives on a hospital trolley, unable to move or speak. But that wasn't what had happened to him, was it? Unless it was going to get worse . . .

The doctor was still speaking. Paddy made himself calm down and listen. ' – cortex is the part of the brain that decodes the messages from your eyes. Now there's nothing wrong with the eyes themselves –' Thank God, Paddy thought. Thank You God. ' – it's just that the messages they receive don't mean anything to you.'

There was a long pause. Paddy couldn't decide exactly how bad that was, but not knowing didn't stop his mouth filling with acid. 'And that's really bad, is it?' he whispered hoarsely.

Say no, his thoughts screamed at the doctor. Say no – say it'll be okay in the long run.

But the doctor said quietly, 'We don't know. Not yet.' He paused. Get it over, Paddy thought at him. 'But if the bleeding inside your head isn't absorbed quickly enough, we're going to have to operate.'

On his brain. His *brain* . . . 'And if you don't?'

'There's a chance of brain damage and you could lose your sight for good,' the doctor said.

Paddy caught his breath. 'No bullshit,' he murmured.

'No bullshit,' the doctor agreed. 'But,' he went on quickly, 'there *is* a chance – and it's a very good chance – but you've got to help me. Now, if you see any flashing lights, or if you feel drowsy or nauseous, you ring for help. If you want a drink, you ring for help. If you need the bathroom – '

'I ring for help,' Paddy finished for him. It was worse than a prison sentence. At least with a jail term there were exercise periods and a prospect of parole.

'That's right,' the doctor said. 'Because the best way to cure this is to do absolutely *nothing*.'

'Okay,' Paddy said at last. 'What now?'

'Now I get the nurse to give you a jab and you go to sleep.' Sleep would be a blessing, Paddy thought – as long as he didn't dream. 'Right,' the doctor said. Paddy heard him get up. 'I'll leave you to it.' He slapped Paddy lightly on the arm.

'See you, doc,' Paddy said, and thought, as long as I can still crack a joke, maybe I'll be okay. Maybe, maybe, maybe . . .

'Corporal Garvey, if I have anything to do with it, you surely will.' Paddy could hear the smile in the man's voice.

The door clicked open and then shut, and Paddy was alone in the dark. 'Good night,' he said softly. 'Sleep tight.'

The jab the nurse gave him put him right out, but he dreamed of Nancy: that she was walking through the rain towards him, and try as he might he could not see her face. He called her name but she did not answer, and he realized that it might not be her at all. How could he tell if he couldn't see her? And then he was on a street in Bosnia, with masonry falling all around. There was a woman carrying a child, hurrying from a standpipe to the shelter of the buildings. A chunk of masonry fell on her and she went down. Sunlight glinted silver on a sniper's rifle sight, and then he was running towards her, heart pounding, breath coming in gasps. Her child cried out, and he reached them, swept them along in his mad headlong dash. They fetched up against the side of the building, and the woman turned. It was Nancy. 'I don't need you, Paddy Garvey,' she said . . .

He woke. He felt his eyelids flicker open, and felt the warmth of the sun on his face. But he could see nothing, just the same greyness as yesterday. He groped for the bell, and the nurse came and fed him and took him to the toilet, then cleaned him up and got him changed into a clean pair of pyjamas.

He felt much better – a bit stronger, and not so ill. But having everything done for him made him feel like a kid. And like a kid, he soon got bored. He wasn't even allowed a radio to pass the time.

Sometime that morning, he heard a familiar voice

out in the corridor, and a few moments later Captain Kate Butler walked in.

'Miss Butler!' Paddy said when the nurse announced her. She'd been the company's assistant adjutant until a year or so ago, until she'd moved to work at headquarters in London, in the public relations department. She was also Major Voce's fiancée.

'In the wars again, Paddy?' she asked.

'Got in the swim of things when I shouldn't, Ma'am,' he said. It was an awful joke, but the best he could manage.

'Poor Paddy – quite the hero though, what with first Bosnia and now this.' She sounded sorry for him, and he hated it.

'Thank you, Miss Butler,' Paddy said, hoping he didn't sound too resentful.

The bed shifted as she sat down on it. Paddy squirmed sideways to make room for her. 'Do you want me to contact anyone at home?' she asked. She was changing the subject, so she probably had guessed.

'No, I don't think so, Ma'am,' Paddy answered. He stared in what he guessed was her general direction, willing her face to come into focus; but there was nothing there.

'What – not even your mum?' She sounded shocked. 'I'd call her for you – '

'No!' Paddy snapped. He tried to soften it, 'Thank you, Ma'am, but she'd worry herself sick.'

Miss Butler never had been one for giving up. She

didn't now. 'Look, I'm here. I've got nothing to do – my holiday plans are on hold. So if you need me, you know where I am.'

It was good of her to offer, Paddy thought. He really shouldn't get the hump with her. 'What happened to Major Voce?' he asked, as much to get her off the subject of helping him as anything else.

'He's a bit tied up at the moment – so near and yet so far,' she said. Her voice had grown warmer.

'Absence makes the heart grow fonder, hey?' Paddy said.

'Yes, it does,' Miss Butler said. She sounded wistful.

Paddy wished, suddenly, that absence had done the trick for him and Nancy – that she would come walking through the door with her impish smile and her bright eyes, ready with a joke to cheer him up. 'Are you smiling, Ma'am?' he asked.

'No!' She sounded guilty.

'It's all right, you can,' he said. 'I am happy for you.'

It was true. It was himself he felt sorry for.

A few minutes later, Miss Butler left to get an English newspaper so she could read the news and sports results out to him.

While she was gone, the nurse – herself a corporal in the Royal Alexandra Nursing Corp – served him lunch. That actually meant she fed him, forkful by forkful. It drove him mad. He had a vision of himself gawping like a baby, waiting for his mum to put a spoonful of mush in his open mouth. Worse, he had a

81

vision of himself as an old man, still needing to be fed.

'I can't feed you if you don't open your mouth,' the nurse said.

'Do me a favour,' Paddy exploded. 'I can't see, but that's all that's wrong with me!' The door clicked open as he added, 'I'm not a bloody baby!' It was as much as he could do not to sweep the damned tray off the bed on to the floor.

Heels clicked on the vinyl.

'We're not having a very good day at all,' the nurse said to whoever had come into the room.

'Right, Paddy Garvey.' It was Miss Butler's voice. Paddy felt himself go crimson because she'd heard his tantrum, even though he was glad she'd come back. 'You're under orders. Give him the fork, Corporal.'

The nurse snorted, but she took his hand and put the fork into it. He could almost feel her displeasure radiate off her. She walked away, heels clicking angrily on the floor.

'Now,' Miss Butler said. 'You've got fish fingers, chips and peas. What do you fancy?'

'I'll have a "p" please, Bob,' Paddy said. He was surprised to find that he was smiling.

They played pin the tail on the donkey with Paddy's mouth and his dinner for a while. Then Miss Butler said, 'This must be pretty boring for you, Paddy.'

'Yep,' he said after he'd swallowed his mouthful of fish finger – the peas were still a bit beyond him. 'I've been going spare with nothing to do but stare at these four walls –' he laughed, a short unpleasant sound.

'Tell you what,' Miss Butler said, 'I'll see what I can do – find out if I can get them to let some of your mates in –'

'Would you, Ma'am? That would be great.'

'Think nothing of it. Just promise me you won't bite that poor nurse's head off again.' The smile was back in her voice. Paddy smiled at her, in what he hoped was the right direction.

She was as good as her word. Later that afternoon, Dave, Tony and Eddie arrived.

'Got us building paths on the beach, they have,' Eddie said. 'Well, not him.' Paddy must have looked puzzled, because he explained, 'Dave, I mean. He's had time off for visiting the sea-bed.'

'So what's that all about then?' Paddy asked. They should have been having local leave by now, surely.

'Some tourists complained,' Tony said. He sounded properly disgusted. 'Reckoned we drove the cas-evac vehicle over their jam sandwiches, or something –'

'Yep,' Dave said. He sounded upset. 'Anyway, we had a bit of a whip-round – got you a pressie, mate, and it isn't even Christmas.'

Somebody put something hard on his chest, and then guided his hands to it.

'Portable CD player,' Eddie explained. 'Thought it would keep you company –'

'Yeah,' Dave added. 'Tony wanted to make it a video machine – all heart, he is.'

'Thanks,' Paddy said. 'I'm touched –' and he was. He was embarrassed to realize that tears were pricking his eyes.

'Anyway, Dave's got something he wants to read to you,' Eddie said. 'Go on, Dave.'

There was a rustle of paper. Dave said, 'I wrote this letter, see – but I suppose I'm going to have to read it out.' He cleared his throat. 'Dear Paddy, If it wasn't for you I wouldn't be here to read this letter. I know we've had our rows in the past, but as mates go, you are the best –' he paused. Paddy swallowed. He wanted to tell Dave that it was all right, that he shouldn't worry, but before he could find the words to interrupt, Dave went on, ' – one of the best, anyway. People say that your life flashes before your eyes, but all that flashed before mine was bubbles –'

Paddy did what he always did when things got heavy. Cracked a joke. 'You kept her quiet then –'

'Air bubbles –' Dave said firmly. 'So mate, thanks for waking me from my sleep in the deep. The vibe down there was not too great. I owe you, Paddy. Hope you see me soon. Love, Dave.' He sounded like he was starting to choke up.

Just for once, Paddy couldn't think of a cheap crack, and Tony got there first. 'Steady on, mate. You'll have me on my knees.'

'Nice,' Eddie put in.

Yeah, Paddy thought. It was. He was desperate to get his sight back, but he knew deep down that if the choice were between that and Dave's life, he'd do the same again.

'Well, go on then,' Dave said. 'Show him his other present.'

There was another rustle of paper. 'Here we go,'

Tony said. He put a piece of paper across Paddy's chest. 'Feel your way around this.' He pulled Paddy's hands on to the paper.

'What is it?' Paddy said, curious.

'We traced every sumptuous curve and bobbly bit with the end of a sharpened dart.'

'A braille pin-up!' Paddy said. He laughed for the first time since the accident. In truth, he couldn't tell one curve from another, but he made a great show of caressing the poster. 'That's not bad, that, lads.'

'Fantastic, eh?' Tony said.

'It's bloody marvellous,' Paddy said. 'Give us five minutes on me own then, boys.'

Later, when Paddy was on his own, the nurse brought some flowers in. She held them in front of him.

'They don't smell of anything much, I'm afraid,' she said.

'Yes they do,' he said. They were lilacs. He'd never have been able to tell that before.

'Any change?' she asked.

'No, nothing,' Paddy said. 'Just blackness. Are you doing something?'

'I waved my hand in front of your face,' she said. She sounded apologetic.

'I didn't know,' Paddy said. He couldn't even begin to make it sound cheerful.

Early next morning, they gave him another brain scan. Now that he knew the worst, Paddy wasn't so scared.

Well, not quite. He still found himself gripping the arms of his wheelchair, and he could feel the sweat beading his face despite the air-conditioning. But at least this time he didn't beg for mercy.

Afterwards, McCudden came to see him again. 'You want it straight, no bullshit, right?' he asked.

'Straight, no bullshit,' Paddy agreed. He lay staring into the darkness. It was amazing how small things took up all of his senses. There was, for instance, a minute wrinkle in the sheet under his shoulder blade, and it hurt horribly. He'd have to complain to the management about it.

'Good – because I've got some good news for you,' the doctor said. 'The pressure on your optic nerve is definitely reducing –'

Paddy couldn't keep the excitement out of his voice. 'Then –'

'It's too early to say. Your sight could return any time between now and –'

'Never, doc? No bullshit, remember.' The disappointment was crushing.

'Never – but only if you're very unlucky.' Paddy heard McCudden stand up. 'The best thing you can do is stay calm and keep cheerful. Time will do the rest.'

Paddy nodded. McCudden left, leaving him alone with only the scent of the lilacs Nurse Mitchell had brought him for company.

The peace and quiet couldn't last. He was listening to his new CD player, when gentle hands removed the headphones from his ears. 'You've got some friends,' Nurse Mitchell said.

Paddy concentrated. Without the headphones, he was sure he could hear more than just her breathing. 'I know,' he said at last. 'Be nice if they'd come to see me.' It was a very minor wind-up, but by the shuffling of feet he knew he'd scored.

He heard her walk away. 'Ring if you need rescuing, Paddy,' she said, and closed the door.

Tony whooped. 'Padd-ee,' he said in a falsetto. 'What is it with you and nurses, eh?'

Paddy grinned. He levered himself up using the hook hanging over the bed. The sedative had once again left him feeling a bit woozy, and the lack of exercise wasn't helping.

'Must be my delicate constitution,' he said. Christine, the woman he'd gone out with in Muenster before the King's Own had been posted to Bosnia, had been a nurse.

'She's in love with me, and she's driving herself mad,' Tony said. Paddy giggled. 'Pity I'm not here to capitalize on it.' Tony sighed.

Fat chance, Paddy thought. Tony had had an affair with a local girl when they had been on exercises in New Zealand. It had nearly cost him his marriage, which was terrible because he was crazy about Joy, his wife. 'Got to rush off to the beach, have you?' he murmured. The thought of lazing around on a stretch of sand, with something long and cool and very alcoholic in one hand, a few bikini-clad females wandering around and absolutely no Colour Sergeant Ryan giving him grief was irresistible.

'I wish, mate,' Tony said. 'I'm going back to Germany today — they brought that compensation tribunal forward –' That was bad luck, Paddy thought: mind you, it was Tony's own fault. It took real skill to knock a barn down, even in a Warrior armoured personnel carrier. 'Mind you,' Tony went on. 'I'm going in a real plane – fancy I might wangle myself a bit of the old club class. Soft seats, sweet-smelling stewardesses – not burger-breath gorillas in some RAF boneshaker. Anyway, two days of sun, sea, sand and naked lovelies – nah. I'm not really in-terested, mate.' He didn't sound very convinced.

'Give me Muenster in the rain any day,' Paddy said. Give him anything that wasn't the inside of this hospital room and he'd be a happy man. He suddenly realized that he didn't know whether Tony was alone or not. 'Is Dave here?' he asked.

'Yeah. Course,' Dave muttered. He sounded as miserable as sin.

'Life and soul of the party,' Paddy said. Just what he needed – Dave Tucker on a guilt trip.

'Yeah, well don't worry about it,' Eddie said. 'Don-na'll be arriving soon to keep up the good name of the Tucker household.'

Actually, the next person through the door was Nurse Mitchell, wheeling Paddy's breakfast on a tray. She swung it over the bed, and guided his hands to the cutlery. She'd long since given up trying to feed him, but it would be just his luck if she started to try again with the others around.

'I can do it, I can do –' he said, trying not to snap. Actually, the smell of the fried food made him feel a bit sick, and visitors or no he could happily have curled up and gone to sleep.

'I know,' she said. 'You're not a bloody two year old – ' She pushed the fork into his hands. 'Yell if you get stuck,' she said.

'You giving that lovely girl a hard time, Paddy?' Tony asked.

'I'm not going to answer that on the grounds that I might incriminate myself,' Paddy said.

After that, he had to pay attention to his food – it was his only hope of dealing with it at all. He thought he'd done quite well, but a bit later when Donna came in, she said, 'What is this? Feeding time at the zoo?' Her stilettoes clacked on the vinyl. 'I've seen Macaulay make less mess.' She kissed him on the cheek. The smell of cosmetics and flowery perfume mingled with that of bacon and baked beans.

'Hi, love,' Paddy said. He thought, I actually sound quite cheerful. Amazing what you can do when you try.

'Right, you lot,' said Nurse Mitchell's voice. 'Out of here in two minutes.'

'I've only just got here,' Donna said, aggrieved.

'I'm sorry,' the nurse said, without sounding sorry at all. 'Corporal Garvey's going to have his bath.'

'Will you be scrubbing his back, Corporal?' Tony asked. Paddy could just imagine the look on his face.

Nurse Mitchell sounded amused. 'I will be scrubbing his *everything*,' she said.

Paddy waited until the sounds of her retreating footsteps told him she'd gone. Then he reached out and grabbed Donna. He pulled her towards him, though it took just about all his strength. 'What does she look like, Donna?' he whispered urgently. Well, his luck had to change sometime.

'Oh,' Donna considered. 'Got dark hair. Lovely eyes. Nice figure. Proper job. Probably single.' She paused. 'I hate her.'

'All right, everyone,' said Nurse Mitchell. 'Time's up.' The rubber of her gloves snapped as she pulled them on.

'I'll wait outside,' Dave said.

Paddy frowned. Something was up.

'Dave – ' Donna said, warningly.

'I'm not going anywhere, all right, Donna?' Something was definitely wrong there, and it didn't sound like the usual situation-normal-all-fouled-up Dave and Donna carry-on. No doubt someone would tell him if he asked. At a guess it was something to do with the business with Kelly and her local boyfriend, though judging from something Dave had said earlier, that had been sorted out at the cost of a massive row between her and Donna.

Eddie came over and grabbed his hand. 'Won't be long,' he said. Paddy only hoped he was right.

Donna kissed him on the cheek. 'Bye pet,' she said. He hugged her and she went out too.

'I'll see you back in the Fatherland,' Tony said. He put an arm round Paddy's shoulder. Paddy fumbled for his hand and gave it a squeeze. 'Take care of yourself, all right?'

'All right,' Paddy said, but he could already feel the good cheer ebbing out of him. Tony walked away.

Keep smiling, Garvey, Paddy told himself. At least until you're sure they've all left.

The bath was fun, and Paddy even managed to persuade Nurse Mitchell to tell him her first name – Sinead – but after that there wasn't much to do except doze while listening to his grand total of three CDs over and over again. It had been nice to see the guys, but he was missing Nancy, and even finding out that Donna reckoned Sinead's looks only made him more miserable. He wanted to decide for himself if she had nice eyes – and a nice figure. He found himself swinging between a fantasy of getting his sight back and wining and dining her by candle-light under a crescent moon; and one of Nancy hearing what had happened. That was it – she'd hear and coming tearing over to see him. At first he wouldn't want to let her in, but he'd relent. She'd hold his hand, kiss him – and he'd close his eyes, only to find, when he opened them, that he could see her: those dark eyes, the smile that made his heart sing . . .

Suddenly the music blared in his ears. 'Shit!' he yelled.

'Sorry,' Dave's voice said from somewhere to his left. 'Sorry.'

Bloody hell, Paddy thought. He must have sneaked in without Sinead noticing. 'What do you want?' he demanded. It might not have been much of a fantasy, but it was all his and he resented it being taken away.

'Just listen,' Dave said. He sounded intense – not at all his usual self. 'I just wanted you to know if – ' he paused. 'If what's happened doesn't get better, I'll look after you.'

'Well, that's a spur to recovery,' Paddy said. He'd

91

meant it to come out light-hearted, but his voice was full of bitterness.

'Me and Donna – together we'll look after you.'

He really means it, Paddy thought – him and Donna? It would be like living in the middle of a live firing exercise – the bullets might not be meant to hit, but they'd do one hell of a lot of damage anyway. 'What does Donna think about this, Dave?' he asked, though he could just imagine.

'She doesn't know yet,' Dave admitted.

'Then I wouldn't bother mentioning it,' Paddy said. ''Cause she'll think you're even more cracked than usual.'

'You've got to be prepared, Paddy,' Dave said earnestly. 'You've got to look at the worst that can happen here – '

Tapping round town with a white stick; trying to look cool in dark glasses on a winter's day; relying on a labrador called Goldie that knows which bus stop to get off the bus at: the thoughts he'd spent two days avoiding tumbled through his mind. If he were lucky he might learn to drink a pint without slopping it down himself. He hauled himself up on his pillows. 'What are you like?' he demanded. 'It's bad enough lying here in the dark like a spare prick, without you reminding me I might have to spend the rest of my life like this.' Suddenly furious, he reached out and found Dave's shirt. He grabbed it and hauled the smaller man closer. 'I'm going to get better, Dave, you under-stand – ' He was shouting, but he didn't care. 'That's all I want to hear. Now if you don't like it, don't bother coming and seeing me – '

'I just thought –' Dave began.

'You thought?' Paddy cut in. 'You thought – sod off!' He pushed Dave away, hard.

The door clicked open. He heard Sinead's footsteps approach, as distinctive as her voice. 'Take it easy, take it easy,' she said, shoving him gently back against the pillows. 'Out,' she said. That must be to Dave. Well good for you, he thought at her. He took a deep breath. His heart was pounding. 'Okay, now, just calm down,' she said. As he heard Dave leave she took his wrist in her hand. 'I'm going to take your pulse,' she said.

The door shut, not gently.

Nice one, Garvey, Paddy thought. You've lost your wife, your sight and probably your career. That's friend number one gone. Much more of this and you won't have anything left to worry about because you won't have anything left to lose.

Dave might have left with his tail between his legs, but it didn't take him long to come back. Paddy had dozed off again, but had woken up again needing a leak, and rung for Sinead to help him. The door opened. Before he could say anything, Dave spoke.

'It's all right – I've got permission from Nursie,' he said from the doorway. 'They've got some kind of emergency going on – like a scene out of M.A.S.H. out there, it is.' He walked in and settled himself somewhere near the bed.

'Oh aye,' Paddy said. He wished he could see the expression on Dave's face – he couldn't tell whether he should say something about the row or not. Not, he decided, after a minute. The trouble was, he couldn't think of anything else to talk about – it wasn't as if he'd had a wild half hour since they'd had the row.

Neither of them said anything. The break in the conversation got so long it was plain embarrassing.

'Tell you what, Paddy,' Dave said after so long Paddy was beginning to wonder if he'd sneaked off. 'You're missing all the excitement out in the big wide world – '

'I think I could have figured that one out, Dave,' Paddy said. He sounded more sarcastic than he'd intended. 'Go on, then,' he said, when Dave didn't continue.

'Well, there's big news and little news and none of it's good news – '

Paddy sighed. 'Get on with it, Dave.'

'Well, the little news is that our Major Voce is being a naughty boy – playing away, he is, with that chopper pilot – '

'You are joking!' Paddy said. Rumours had been flying around the camp ever since the night of the officers' last big bash – a member of the catering corps had seen Voce wandering outside the officers' mess with a drop-dead gorgeous RAF pilot, and the news had spread like wildfire.

''Strue,' Dave said. 'Got a mate working in Brucie's office – ' that was Lieutenant Forsythe – 'but anyway, that's the little bit of bad news. The big bad news'll blow your socks off – ' he paused. 'Course, I could do with a cuppa right now – '

'Get on with it, Dave,' Paddy said, not caring that he was rising to the bait.

'It looks like Tony might not make his compo tribunal after all,' Dave said.

Paddy shoved himself up in the bed. 'How'd he wangle that, then?' Paddy asked, interest aroused. For everything he might say, Tony was the last man in the King's Own to go doing anything that might harm his career.

'He's got himself made a guest of the Cypriot police force,' Dave said.

'Pull the other one.' As wind-ups went, it was nowhere – far too outrageous to be convincing.

'It's true,' Dave said. 'Hey, do you think Nursie'll miss her rubber gloves?'

'What?' There was an odd squeaking sound.

'Made a fishy,' Dave said. 'Give you something to look forward to – for when you can see again, like.' More squeaking noises. 'There you go – nice fat body and floppy finger fins.' He grabbed Paddy's hands and pushed something round and wobbly into them.

'Give over, Dave,' Paddy said. 'And tell us about Tony.'

'Told you – he's a guest of the Cypriot police. Got caught with an antique Greek bracelet at the airport. He got it off Marsha Stubbs and *she* got it off that local bloke whose house they've been staying in – told her it was repro.'

'I don't follow,' Paddy said. It sounded like the sort of wild thing Donna would get up to, not calm, sensible Mrs Stubbs.

'She had some idea about importing them into Germany — she was going to take the orders, he was going to fill them.'

It started to make sense. 'Only it was strictly one-off,' he finished for Dave, 'because it was just a way to smuggle the originals in.'

'Got it in one, Einstein. Only my Donna's making like Emma Peel — says she's going to fix this Andreas bloke, and Eddie's doing a Steed impersonation —'

'So Tone's in the slammer, Mrs Stubbs is about to join him, and Donna and Horatio are chasing the naughty Greek?'

'Correct,' Dave said.

'Been a big hit, then, Cyprus. Hasn't it?' Paddy said.

'I'll be devastated to leave.' Suddenly Dave sounded embarrassed again.

Oh shit, Paddy thought. We are going to have to talk about it. Otherwise it's just going to keep coming back. He shut his eyes. The strange thing was how doing that changed the darkness. With his eyes open, there was a scary kind of greyness. With them closed, the darkness became somehow comforting. He'd decided it was because he knew to expect it.

'Listen mate,' Paddy said awkwardly. 'I'm sorry I laid into you like I did.' He really wanted to explain that he meant everything he said, but just not the way it had come out: that he needed to know that all his mates were pulling for him, and hadn't written him off. But he knew it would get complicated, and he just didn't have the energy. 'It was stupid.'

'No,' Dave said. 'I shouldn't have said anything. I was stupid.'

No, Paddy thought. Just feeling guilty. He didn't need to hear Dave say it – he could imagine how he'd have felt. 'Well, that's one all in the stupid stakes, then,' he said. That seemed to cover it. He cast around for something to change the subject, but everything he could think of was totally morbid or maudlin or both.

Dave saved him the effort. 'I'll tell you what,' he whispered from close to Paddy's left ear. 'She fancies the bedpan off you, that nurse.'

This was better. 'Sinead,' Paddy said smugly.

'Sinead,' Dave repeated. 'Nice name, you lucky so and so.'

'Yeah well –' Paddy said. Thinking about her suddenly reminded him that he'd rung for her ages ago to help him take a leak. 'Dave,' he said, trying not to sound embarrassed.

'Yeah?' Dave sounded wary, as if he thought Paddy was going to start talking about the row again.

Paddy let him stew in it for a second. Then he said, 'I'm gagging for a pee.'

If Paddy was embarrassed, it wasn't anything to the way it made Dave feel by the sound of his voice. 'Right,' he muttered. 'Where's the uh . . . the uh . . . whatsit?'

'Under the bed, it should be,' Paddy said. He pointed downwards.

Dave moved around. 'It's not under the bed, Paddy,' he said. 'Any ideas?'

Oh for pity's sake, Paddy thought. He was getting a bit desperate. 'Over there in the purple cupboard?' He pointed in the general direction of the far corner.

'What?' Dave sounded bemused.

'I'm blind,' Paddy shouted. 'I don't bloody know, do I?' If he couldn't have a leak soon he was going to have to try his hand at blindfolded knot tying, that was what he did know.

'Don't worry, I'll find it!' Dave sounded affronted. 'Just you point Percy. I may love you but I do not want Sinead to think I covet your conjugals.'

'Just hurry up, Dave, will you?' If he didn't, Sinead was going to be in for a spot of bed changing.

He heard Dave go out, banging the door behind him. He came back a moment later. 'Okey dokey,' Dave said.

Paddy pulled himself into a sitting position. The sedation was beginning to wear off, but he still felt as weak as a kitten. 'This is going to be embarrassing,' he said. At least he wouldn't be able to see Dave blush.

'Don't worry, relief is at hand,' Dave said, deadpan.

'Where?' Paddy asked, preparing to grope his way to the bedpan.

'Down the corridor,' Dave said.

It might as well have been in Muenster. 'Oh no,' Paddy said. 'I can't do that.' It wasn't just the fact that he could barely move. He was terrified of doing anything that would set his chances of recovery back.

'Suit yourself,' Dave said. He started to whistle. Paddy heard him pace across the floor.

There was a sudden whoosh of running water. It made Paddy need to pee so bad it hurt. 'You sod,' Paddy said. He rolled over towards Dave and reached out to him. 'Give us a hand then.'

Paddy stood up. He put his arm round Dave's shoulder, thinking he'd just need a bit of support. But his legs almost gave way beneath him. With Dave guiding him, he stumbled to the door. He felt the jamb under his groping hands. 'Shit, my legs feel like jelly,' he said. The thought of walking, blind as he was, down the corridor suddenly seemed like running a marathon blindfolded.

'Well, it's understandable,' Dave said. 'They have been out of service for a while. Don't worry – you'll be able to sprint back.' He paused. 'Left turn.'

Walking down the corridor was terrifying. Dave went at a real lick, and Paddy had to steel himself not to ask to slow down. He couldn't get away from the feeling that at any moment he might be about to put his foot in a hole or slam into something. There was only the feel of Dave's shoulder under his arm to re-assure him. He put his hand out and trailed it against the wall. It helped a little – helped him to know that something existed in the universe outside of himself.

'Door ahead,' Dave said. 'Be so good as to open it, my good man,' he added in a fake posh accent.

Paddy stretched his hand out. He touched the flat surface of the door, and then his groping fingers found the smooth coldness of the handle. Push or pull, he wondered: he'd just remembered that it would be a swing door so trolleys could get through it from both directions, when a woman's voice from behind said, 'Paddy!' in an imperious tone.

Sinead! he thought. Oh shit. He swung round, pushing Dave ahead of him. Something shoved him hard from behind and he went sprawling. He got his hands up in front of his face, but his foot turned and he did a bad imitation of a shoulder roll. His head slammed into the floor. From a great distance he heard someone say, 'I didn't see him coming through – ', and feet running – an alarm bell clanging – and Dave muttering. 'Paddy. Oh *fuck* – Paddy?'

Then the voices faded and there was only silence and darkness, and then nothing at all.

The jolting of the trolley beneath his back woke Paddy. They were going at a hell of a pace. He felt sick and dizzy and it took him a minute to work out what had happened. He stared up into the unending greyness. I fell, he thought. They told me to rest but I had to go swanning off with Dave . . . He wondered how much time he'd lost. Must be on my way to emergency, he thought – they'd be going slower if they were taking him back to his room. He'd have asked, but he couldn't be sure if anyone was close enough to hear, and he'd have felt like a prat if there wasn't.

There was a confusion of bangs and clicks, and then the distinct sound of a lift door opening.

'I'm sorry, Fusilier – you can't come with him,' said a female voice Paddy didn't recognize.

'Please,' Dave's voice said out of the darkness. He sounded on the edge of tears.

100

'It's all right, mate,' Paddy said or tried to say – he couldn't be sure whether the words had actually left his throat. 'I'll be fine. I'll be fine.' He only wished he believed it.

But incredibly it turned out to be true. After the inevitable scan – which this time almost seemed routine – Sinead helped the technician move Paddy from the machine back to his trolley. There was an unbearable knot of tension in his belly, and his hands were clenched so hard he could feel his nails bite into his palms. He felt her hands on both sides of his head. They were cool and gentle, yet firm. 'Well, Paddy,' she said, 'It seems some parts of your head are thicker than others – there's no additional damage.'

'Thank God,' Paddy said. He swallowed hard. The tension drained out of him. Then he remembered the desperation he'd heard in Dave's voice as he was left behind outside the lift. Christ, he thought – if it gets back to McCudden that Dave was helping me to the bog when I fell, Voce is bound to hear about it. Dave'll be for the high-jump again. 'Listen,' he said. 'It wasn't Dave's fault.' He thought, the poor sod was only trying to help because he felt guilty – same as when he decided to plan my future for me.

'I've sent him out to get some air,' Sinead said. She sounded amused.

Paddy licked his lips. 'Listen,' he said, 'Could you hang around for a while, please?'

'Sure,' Sinead said softly. Her fingers smoothed his hair.

Dave's right, Paddy thought. She does fancy me.

Under the circumstances, he hardly liked to point out that he still wanted a pee.

Sinead stayed for quite a while, but then Dave came back and she said she had to go. That was fair enough, but Dave had only popped in to say he thought he ought to go and stop Donna doing a Modesty Blaise impersonation all over the island.

After that, it was back to the CD player. He gave it up when he realized he could almost lip-synch to every track – even the ones he hated. After that there was nothing to do but sit and stare into the greyness, and will himself to see something. Once, he thought he saw a faint barring of light on the darkness, but it went as soon as he concentrated on it. I should tell someone, he thought. But Major McCudden had said to ring if he saw flashes of light, and this was nothing like that exciting. But still . . . he reached for the bell. His hand hesitated over it. There's no point, he thought. All it'll get me is being poked around again, and anyway it's gone now. If it comes back, I'll tell Sinead.

So he sat there, willing it to happen.

It didn't.

The door opened suddenly. The noise made him jump. 'Hello?' he said, tentatively.

'Corporal Garvey? It's Captain Butler.'

The sound of her voice cheered him up immediately, but he said, 'Oh dear.' He paused. 'I mean, "hello, Ma'am".'

She walked towards the bed. The sound of paper

rattling overlay that of her footsteps. 'What do you mean, "Oh dear"?' She sounded amused. He heard her put something down on the bedside table.

'Must be bad if they sent an officer,' he explained.

'They didn't send her, she came of her own free will,' Miss Butler said. Again, paper rustled. 'And she's brought you some fruit.' There was the sound of running water.

'Well, that's very nice of her,' Paddy said. He hoiked himself upright.

'Hasn't Major Voce been in?' She sounded surprised.

'Not today,' Paddy said. 'I think he's got enough on his plate.'

'Really?' Miss Butler said. Again, she sounded surprised.

Paddy knew she was visiting on leave, but he was surprised she was that far out of the loop. 'Haven't you heard? Tony Wilton's been arrested at the airport with twenty thousand quid's-worth of antique jewellery stuffed down his Y-fronts.'

'You're joking!' Miss Butler exclaimed.

'Only about the Y-fronts,' Paddy admitted. 'All in all it hasn't been a very happy island for Major Voce,' he added sombrely; and, he thought, I've been at the back of a couple of his big problems – first screwing up the Fibua exercise, and then managing to get myself in here. The way his luck's been going, it's a wonder we even managed to save that woman in the car crash – she'll never know what a close shave she had.

The bed moved as Miss Butler sat down on it. 'No,' she agreed. 'It hasn't.' There was an edge to her voice. Uh-oh, Paddy thought. The beautiful chopper pilot. Evidently news travelled as fast through the officers' mess as it did through the Naafi.

But Major Voce was a damn sight better off than he might have been – he had the one thing that would have helped Paddy get through. 'Still,' he said, 'you're here, Miss Butler, so I guess that'll be some compensation for him, hey?'

She gave a long, ragged sigh, but didn't answer.

'Isn't it?' Paddy asked, puzzled.

'Yeah,' she said. 'I suppose so.' She didn't sound convinced.

Keep stumm, Garvey, Paddy told himself. They're officers. Don't get involved. But he said, 'Something the matter, Ma'am?'

'Yes,' she said, pointedly. 'And I think you know what it is – you and the rest of B Company.'

'Those magnificent women in their flying machines?' he asked, trying to keep his voice light.

Bad move. 'Oh Garvey!' Miss Butler said, sounding disgusted.

'Sorry, Ma'am,' Paddy said, and realized he didn't sound at all repentant. 'But that is what it's all about, isn't it?'

There was an uncomfortable silence. 'Well, yes,' Miss Butler finally admitted.

Now what the hell do I say, Paddy thought. Then it occurred to him that the truth would do no harm at all. 'Well,' he said. 'I'm sure there's nothing in it,

104

Ma'am, because it's obvious to all of us that he is completely nuts about you.' She didn't say anything. Paddy thought, this is no good. She isn't hearing what I'm saying, and if I can't make her she'll make a mistake both of them will regret for the rest of their lives. He cast around for another way of putting it, but he had to take a deep, ragged breath before he could bring himself to speak. 'I was faithful to Nancy all through our marriage –' Just for an instant he saw her in his mind's eye: laughing eyes and a dark wing of hair, and above all that impish smile. It was enough to make his eyes burn, but he managed to continue. 'And what a brilliant success that was.'

'Are you saying it's all right for him to play around?' Her voice was dangerous.

'No, no,' Paddy said quickly. 'It's just –' he groped for the right words, realizing Miss Butler was losing patience with him. 'Whatever he's done, is it really worth losing everything for?'

'Oh I don't know.' She sighed and shifted in her seat, making the sheets rustle. 'I don't know what I think any more.'

Last chance, Garvey, Paddy told himself. 'I just think, if you've found the right person you should do everything you can to hold on to them.' Again, he saw Nancy, this time the way she'd looked when she finally said yes to his proposal – the fourth time he'd made it. 'I didn't,' he said. 'And I wish I had.'

After that, he didn't say any more. There wasn't anything left *to* say.

By the time Sinead came in with his tea, he'd thought

105

things through a bit, and decided that the only hope for him was to take his chances where he found them. He was allowed up to eat at the table now, and he waited till he'd finished and Sinead was helping him back to bed.

Then he went for it. 'Sinead,' he said, 'would you do me a favour?'

'Sure,' she said. Her hands on his back were firm and reassuring.

'Would you come and visit me out of uniform –' he didn't know why that mattered so much, given that he couldn't see her. 'You know,' he explained, 'when you're off duty?'

'Are you inviting me out?' she asked. She sounded amused.

'Well,' he considered. 'I'm inviting you in, really,' he said. He felt suddenly shy and vulnerable; he realized it was because he couldn't see her face. All he had to go on was her tone of voice, and he couldn't tell whether she was laughing at him or with him.

'It'd be a pleasure,' she said, putting him out of his misery.

He couldn't stop himself from grinning. 'How about tonight?' he asked, and swung his legs up on to the bed.

'Fine,' she said. She sounded delighted.

'I'll pick you up about eight then?'

She just laughed, and a moment later the door clicked as she left.

The venetian blind clattered as Sinead closed it.

Paddy looked over to where he knew she must be standing. 'That's very nice,' he said, though he had no idea what she was wearing.

Her heels clacked on the vinyl. She's wearing high heels, he thought. The idea pleased him – that she'd bothered to dress up, even though she knew he couldn't see.

'So where are you taking me, Paddy Garvey?' she asked.

Out of the wide range of places available? he thought wryly to himself. But he'd come up with a line to cover this one while he'd been waiting. 'I thought we'd start with a tour of Sinead Mitchell – the life and times.'

She giggled. 'Been there before, I'm afraid.' Her voice was low and husky.

'But never in such charming company,' Paddy said. He was feeling more cheerful than he had in days.

'Don't joke – it might be true,' she said. She leaned closer, bringing with her the scent of musk and roses. Her hand pushed at his leg.

'What?' he said, taken by surprise.

'Move over,' she said. He felt the bed give a bit as she sat down.

'What are you doing?' he demanded, but he knew full well.

The next moment, her arm was round his shoulder, and he could feel her legs rubbing the length of his. She took his hand in hers. 'If you think I'm sitting on that chair all evening you've got another think coming.'

'What if someone comes in?' Paddy asked, shocked.

'I'm a nurse, aren't I?' Sinead said.

'Yeah,' Paddy answered. 'I suppose you are.' It was a bit more restrained than the other answer that came to mind, which was 'delightful.'

'Besides, I fixed it with the other girls,' she said. 'Green they were – the vixens.' She stroked his shoulder with her free hand. 'Are you comfy?'

He covered her hand with his own larger one. 'Yeah,' he said. 'I suppose I am.' It wasn't actually the word he would have chosen, but in polite company he guessed it was as good as any other. 'I'll have to go private more often.'

She laughed, and moved in closer. 'You've handled this really well, you know, Paddy,' she said.

'I'm not sure about that,' he answered. 'There've been times I thought I'd top myself – I mean, if this is permanent.' She breathed in sharply and squeezed his hand. 'It's okay,' he said, thinking, you clot, Garvey – just what every girl wants on a first date: a declaration of intent to commit suicide. 'I soon got over it.'

'What's it like?' she asked. 'I can't imagine it at all.'

He considered. 'Well,' he said slowly. 'It's like a patrol on a really black night. Everything else is sharpened – hearing, smell, touch.' He found that he didn't really want to talk about it. She was far too distracting. He took her free hand in both of his, and began to stroke it. 'It's like your hand, for example – it's like stroking a cat.'

She laughed. 'Thank you,' she said, sounding a

little bit embarrassed. Paddy found that quite charming.

She stroked his hand in turn. 'Yours are like an old stone wall,' she said.

'Worker's hands – proud of it,' he said, only putting it on for her benefit a little.

'What about this?' she asked. She moved his hands to her face, and his fingers drifted gently down her cheek.

'Nice,' she said. The word was thoroughly inadequate.

'And this?' she asked, and kissed him, soft as a butterfly's wing, on his temple.

He didn't say anything, just turned his head and kissed her. He almost missed her mouth, but the next kiss found her lips briefly; and the one after that lasted a deliciously long time. He closed his eyes. That way, he could almost imagine that everything was normal, that he couldn't see so he could concentrate on the softness of her lips, the silky texture of her hair beneath his hand, the velvet smoothness of her skin.

He pulled away at last, because he wanted to tell her that she pleased him very much. His eyes opened. Something white floated in front of them. He blinked and shook his head, ignoring Sinead's concerned questions. The whiteness came into focus.

Her face. Her beautiful, beautiful face. 'Are they blue or green?' he said, staring into her eyes

And then she was laughing, and he was; and that was the end of their date because she went off to get Major McCudden.

'All I can say is, there seems to have been an emotional component to it,' the Major said after he had examined Paddy.

'What?' Paddy asked, looking guiltily at Sinead. She was still in civvies, and not looking too comfortable about it.

'You got happy,' McCudden said. He glanced at Sinead. 'Or perhaps just very relaxed. Either way, it seems someone was doing a good job.' He started towards the door. Paddy watched him, delighting in being able to do it. 'Now, you know what I'm going to say next – get some rest, Corporal.'

Dave, Tony and Eddie walked through the door. 'Hi, Paddy,' Dave said.

Paddy stared fixedly at the far wall. 'Hi Dave,' he replied. 'Is Horatio here?'

'Yeah mate,' Eddie said. 'And Tony.'

Tony wiggled his ears with his hands. Paddy managed to keep a straight face. 'Hello, Paddy,' he said in a silly voice.

'Great,' Paddy said. He couldn't quite keep from smiling, but he thought he had them fooled. 'What'd you do? Dig a tunnel?'

'Got out last night, mate,' Tony answered. His voice was suddenly serious, and Paddy knew it was working. 'It's a bit of a mystery, but they caught the Greek wide-boy with the goodies in the back of the car and he put his hands up.'

Paddy was hard put to decide who looked more embarrassed – Dave or Eddie. In the end, it was Dave who spoke. 'My Donna planted them on him – '

'With a bit of help from Major Voce's fiancée,' Eddie added. He didn't know Miss Butler – she'd left the regiment before he'd joined. 'She distracted him so Donna could get at his car.'

'Well good for her,' Paddy said. He wondered how she and the major were getting on. He hoped she'd forgiven him.

'Anyway,' Tony said. 'How's life in the fast lane, Paddy?'

'Oh you know Tone. Terrible and horrible and –'

'Paddy?' Sinead said. 'Catch!' She chucked a can of lager at him.

He caught it one-handed. The others' eyes widened. 'And bloody marvellous!' he finished. He popped the can.

Eddie was the first to get it. 'Ace!' he exclaimed.

'What?' Paddy said. 'Did you think you were going to Germany without me?' He took a long pull on the can. 'Drink,' he said. He was laughing, so that lager ran down his chin and on to his singlet. 'Drink – you too, Eddie. Nurse's orders!'

Sinead slipped away. Just as she was going out the door, she caught his eye. He raised his can in a toast to her.


But as it turned out, the lads did go back to Germany without him. Major Voce came to see him later that morning.

Paddy did his best to come to attention while sitting in bed.

'At ease, Corporal,' the major said. 'I've spoken to

111

Major McCudden,' he said once he had asked how Paddy was feeling, 'and he says you need time to recover properly. I'm recommending a full month's convalescence in England –'

'Thank you, Sir,' Paddy said, although he was eager to get back into the swing of things.

'And I've decided that while you're over there, you might as well go straight on to your Platoon Sergeant's Battle Course,' Major Voce went on. 'It's about time – you did very well in Bosnia; and though that first Fibua exercise was nothing more than a shambles, you more than made up for it when you rescued Tucker.'

'Yes, Sir,' Paddy said. 'Thank you, Sir.'

Major Voce walked over to the door. He opened it, and Paddy saw that Miss Butler was waiting for him outside. She murmured something to the major, then came into the room and shut the door behind her.

'Thank you, Paddy,' she said.

'Think nothing of it, Ma'am,' he answered.

She left and he got up and went to look out of the window. After a moment, he saw her and Major Voce come out. They were holding hands.

'Thank you, Miss Butler,' he said aloud. And then he added, 'Goodbye, Nancy. It was good knowing you.'

# Chapter 5

Paddy got back from his Platoon Sergeant's Battle Course to find that Dave had got caught impersonating an officer – he'd been conned into it by Lieutenant Forsythe, who was trying to win a bet – but being Dave instead of getting chucked out, he'd been put on extra duties. CSM Stubbs had had a bit of a breakdown, from stress left over from the tour in Bosnia and been given time off. And Donna, of all people, had started to help the colonel's wife with her art exhibitions.

But more important than any of that, the base was about to be invaded by America – or rather, a group of American soldiers on an exchange visit. It was to last two weeks, after which the King's Own were to be posted back to the UK, for ceremonial duties at Windsor and Buckingham Palace.

Two Platoon assembled on the parade ground to greet their guests. They climbed out of a civilian coach and formed up along the opposite side of the square. One of the men quickly assembled a standard, which he carried to the front and then held aloft.

Major Voce stood on the steps leading up to the accommodation block. He made a brief speech welcoming them, then gave Tony the order to dismiss the men. As soon as he had done so, Eddie Nelson turned to Paddy.

'Exchange visit?' he asked. He was incredibly excited. 'You mean we get to go to America?'

'That's the idea,' Paddy said. 'They come over here, play at silly buggers for a fortnight – we go over there and do the same.' He slapped Eddie on the shoulder, then wandered off towards the accommodation block.

Major Voce intercepted him. 'Corporal Garvey?'

Paddy turned. 'Sir?'

'How are the eyes?' the major asked.

'Absolutely fine, thank you Ma'am,' Paddy deadpanned.

Fortunately, Major Voce appreciated the joke. He grinned, then said, 'I hear you did well on your Platoon Sergeant's Battle Course.' He folded his arms.

Paddy was delighted with the compliment. There had been times – like when he had stolen the APC, back before they had been posted to Bosnia – when Major Voce had been deeply unimpressed with him. Paddy had worked hard to make him change his opinion, and it seemed to have worked. 'I like to keep my end up, Sir,' he said.

'So I've heard,' the major said. 'It's good to have you back, Garvey.'

'It's good to be back, Sir,' Paddy said as the major walked away.


That night, the Naafi laid on an American theme evening. 'The Boogie-Woogie Bugle Boy of Company

B' blared out of the sound system. A few people were jiving to it, but basically it was hardly the grand welcome promised by the banner slung across the back of the stage. Paddy perched on the back of a chair to watch the proceedings. There wasn't much point in doing anything else – the Yanks had turned the heads of every female on the base, or so it seemed. Eddie, at least, seemed to be getting on okay with them. He was talking to a man-mountain named Mather – Mad Mick, he'd said they called him, and it seemed to fit – and another guy called Jim Gallagher. Earlier, he'd swapped Gallagher his beret for a pair of Ray-ban sunglasses. He was still wearing them, despite the bar's dim lighting.

He left the Americans and came over to Paddy, just as Dave sauntered up bearing a couple of pints. 'Anyone would think there was a shortage of nylons,' he grumbled, handing Paddy his drink.

'No shortage of interest, anyway,' Paddy agreed. He sipped his beer. The Americans had said their base was dry – no alcohol allowed. No wonder they were taking advantage.

'It's the novelty, isn't it?' he said. He gestured at them with his glass of Coke. 'They've got a completely different background – totally different culture and all that.'

Personally, Paddy didn't think they had much in the way of culture, but he didn't say anything. He spotted Donna coming and nudged Dave.

By the way she was looking around, she hadn't spotted them. Before Dave could call her, Mather planted himself in front of her. 'Hey, Beautiful,' he said, holding out his arms. 'Where have you been all my life?'

Paddy had his hand on Dave's arm. He felt the other man tense up.

Donna looked him up and down. 'Avoiding you,' she said in her usual broad Geordie accent.

Dave relaxed slightly, but Paddy could see he was ready to have a go if Mather didn't back off. But the American threw back his head and laughed. He clapped his hands then raced over to Gallagher, and said, 'Hey Jim! Doncha just love these Cockney girls, man?'

By that time, Donna had seen Paddy and the others. She came over. 'Hiya!' she said, and hitched herself up on the table next to Dave.

'What are you doing here?' he demanded.

Oh no, Dave, Paddy thought. It was always the same – one of them would pick a fight over nothing, the other would respond and before you knew it Dave would be kipping on a sofa in the Naafi or Donna would have persuaded Joy to let her stay there for a few days.

'I'm allowed out, aren't I?' Donna snapped. She did have a point, Paddy thought – Dave would have kept her on a very short leash if he could. 'I came to see what all the fuss was about.'

Not a lot, in Paddy's opinion – the music had gone from 'Boogie-Woogie Bugle Boy' to 'Chattanooga Choo Choo' and back to 'Bugle Boy' again. Michael Jackson eat your heart out, he thought. It apparently hadn't occurred to anyone that they could play half the current Top Forty and be playing something American.

'Who's looking after Macaulay?' Dave demanded. Paddy supposed it was a good point – it was just that the answer never seemed to be 'Dave is'.

'Joy,' Donna said. So surprise me, Paddy thought; but he knew better than to stick his nose in. 'She's fine – she's learning her lines for *Pygmalion*.' That was the musical the base amateur dramatics society was putting on to mark the King's Own's return to Blighty.

Mather suddenly broke away from the people he was talking to, rushed up to the stage and pushed the DJ off the sound system. He fiddled with it briefly, then grabbed the microphone. 'Hey Jimbo, boy,' he called. A heavy bass beat began to pound out of the speakers. 'Haul your ass up here – let's show these boys what we're made of, man.'

The track was 'The Walk' by Jimmy McCracklin. As the beat pounded out and the music hotted up, Mather leapt off the stage. He stripped down to his singlet. His heavily muscled shoulders gleamed in the stage lights, which also picked out a tattooed dragon that coiled over his left arm. Gallagher rushed up to join him and the two men went into a funky walk routine to the music. They were good, and so was the music. Paddy found himself swaying in time. People started moving towards the stage to join in, Donna among them.

Mather spotted her. He danced towards her.

'Come on beautiful – you're coming with me.' He reached out and pulled her into the dance. She didn't object. Mather held her hand and showed her the steps, but by now they were only two among many.

Dave scowled.

'Tell you what, Dave,' Eddie said. 'He's a big lad.'

'Didn't they tell you, Eddie?' Dave answered. 'Size is not important.'

Will be if you get his fist in your face, Paddy thought. It didn't seem that unlikely. He suddenly realized that he, Dave and Eddie were the only people in the room who weren't dancing. Some people beckoned to Eddie to come and dance. He raised his hands in acknowledgement and loped off to join them. Dave was still scowling. Oh to hell with him, Paddy thought. He followed Eddie. Donna grinned at him, then pointedly turned round so she wasn't facing Dave. Paddy danced next to her – keeping an eye on her was the least he could do for Dave. And the most he was prepared to do.

Afterwards, Paddy couldn't quite remember how the arm wrestling started, but it pretty soon became a needle match.

He sat opposite Gallagher, right hands locked together, elbows on the table and left arms behind their backs. Each of them had a fiver – his stake money – gripped between his teeth. Candles had been stuck into ashtrays at either end of the table. In their flickering light, Paddy could see the sweat glistening on Gallagher's face. Paddy grinned. So far, he was having an easy time of it.

'Paddypaddypaddy,' yelled Dave and Eddie. Someone, somewhere was pounding a beer mug on the table.

'Go Jimbo. Go Jimbo. Go go go,' Mather yelled.

Paddy felt the tendons in his neck stand out. He poured a little pressure on. Gallagher's hand gave a little. Just a little, but Paddy thought, *Gotcha!* He heaved.

Gallagher grunted. His hand slammed back, inches from the candle. Eddie and Dave and the other Brits cheered and whistled.

Mather slammed his hand down on the table. 'Oh man,' he moaned.

Gallagher grinned good-naturedly and handed over his fiver. Mather grabbed him and pulled him out of his seat. He sat down facing Paddy. 'How about giving Mad Mick a go?' he asked.

Paddy rubbed his arm. Gallagher hadn't been hard to defeat, but he hadn't been a pushover, either. 'Oh no, mate,' he said. 'I'm a bit tired – '

Mather put his arm on the table.

'Go on, Paddy,' Eddie said.

Dave leaned towards him. 'You're a sure bet, Paddy – '

'Have you seen the size of him?' Paddy protested.

'Think of the money,' Dave said.

Good point, Paddy thought. Besides, he was going to lose a lot of face if he didn't. 'Have you got any money?' Paddy asked.

Mather produced a fiver and stuck it in his mouth. He wiggled his fingers.

'Go for it,' someone shouted, though who it was and who they were cheering for Paddy couldn't tell.

Paddy planted his elbow on the table and locked hands with Mather. The American's grip was vice-like. Once they had both put their left hands behind their backs, Gallagher steadied their hands and counted them down. 'Go!' he yelled.

Mather pushed. Paddy matched him. All around him, people were shouting, but he didn't dare pay any attention. He stared at Mather. The pressure on his arm was relentless. He matched it. Tried to put more on. Sweat studded his face. There was a knot of tension at his neck. It's only pain, he thought. Ignore it. He felt his jaw clench.

'You can do it, Paddy,' Dave shouted from behind Mather. Paddy caught his eye. I can't, he thought.

His hand inched back as Mather poured on the pressure. He could see the tendons in the big American's arm flex. I can do this, Paddy thought. I can. Do. This. But his hand went back a little further, and now he could feel the heat of the candle. I can't, he thought. A muscle jumped in his cheek.

And then suddenly Mather slid backwards off his chair and Paddy reflexively slammed his hand down on the table.

'What?' Paddy said. He replayed the scene in his head, and realized he'd seen Dave pull the American's chair out from him.

But by that time Mather had thrown his money on the table and was going for Dave. 'Sonofabitch,' he yelled. Eddie and Gallagher both got in his way.

'Accidents happen, right?' Gallagher said. He pushed Mather back. There was a moment of silence in which anything could have happened. Then he shrugged and walked off. At the last minute, he reached back, stopped and slapped Dave gently on the face a few times.

Unfinished business, Paddy thought. He had a feeling it was going to get pretty damn nasty, sooner or later. He found he didn't care – maybe if the Yank kicked the crap out of Dave he'd finally learn a lesson. He scowled at him as he went to catch Mather. He gave the American his money back and bought him a pint. Then he went back to Dave.

'That was totally out of order, Dave,' he said.

'I was just trying to help, Paddy.' Dave made it sound perfectly logical.

'I didn't want any help.' Paddy managed to keep his temper with difficulty.

Dave didn't get it. 'You were losing!'

'So I was losing? So what?' Paddy demanded. But he knew that Dave hadn't ever quite grasped the idea of competition for its own sake.

Sure enough, he said, 'That's why I was trying to help!' Again, he managed to make it sound the most natural thing in the world.

Paddy gave up. 'I don't know why I bother,' he said as he walked off.

Behind him, he heard Eddie say, 'So much for the friendly exchange.'

Yeah, right, Paddy thought; and he decided to avoid the Americans in general and Mather in particular as much as he could.

Unfortunately, that wasn't as easy as it could have been. Paddy was woken the next morning by the sound of singing from outside the accommodation block.

'Airborne daddy gonna take a little trip.' The voices were massed, male and American.

Paddy looked at his watch. Seven hundred hours. The Americans were mad – not just Mick Mather, the whole lot of them. That morning there was going to be a friendly baseball game, with a barbecue afterwards for lunch, with a cross-country race in 432 armoured personnel carriers and on foot to follow. Paddy was quite looking forward to it, but he was determined to get as much sleep as possible first.

He groaned and rolled over, but it was no good. The sound went on. He lay there with the blanket over his head for a minute, trying to work out where he'd heard it before. Then he realized: just about every American war movie he'd ever seen.

The Americans were training.

He got up and leaned out of the window. Next to him, Eddie did the same. The American platoon came trotting through the trees in front of the accommodation block. The leading man was carrying the flag aloft on a pole, and they were wearing tee-shirts that said 'ARMY' on them. Probably needed to be reminded who they were, Paddy thought.

'Airborne daddy gonna take a little trip,' sang Sergeant Stein.

'Airborne daddy gonna take a little trip,' the platoon sang back at him.

Singing Jodies, the Americans called it. Soft in the head, Paddy called it. He caught Eddie's eye. They grinned at each other. Paddy glanced up and around. They weren't the only ones.

'Stand up, hook up, shuffle to the door,' sang Stein. The platoon echoed it. 'Jump right out and count to four,' he sang, and again the platoon sang it back.

Right, Paddy thought. That's enough of that. He leant down and picked up the jug of drinking water from his bedside table.

'Platoon halt,' shouted Stein. 'Left, left, left right left left –' The platoon marched up to the accommodation block.

Wait for it, Paddy thought. Wait till you can see the whites of their eyes. As one, the windows of the accommodation block banged open. Water from a dozen jugs rained down on the Americans, followed by a couple of toilet rolls and a condom water bomb.

'Way to go, dudes!' someone shouted in a phony American accent.

The American platoon broke up in confusion. They stared up at the windows. Then one of them laughed and most of them joined in.

The baseball was not going well. The baseball was, in fact, a ruddy disaster. Paddy waited in the outfield, or whatever you called it in baseball, hefting the unfamiliar weight of the catcher's mitt on his right hand. Not that he'd had much call to use it yet. Eddie, dressed in cricket whites, was pitching – in this case to Mather. The big American bounced slightly on his toes. Eddie wound it up and threw the ball, having finally got the hang of not having a run up.

Mather grinned and slugged the ball. It whistled straight at Paddy. He got ready for it, ignoring the cheers and whistles of the watching Americans as Mather dashed round the bases. It was there . . . it was . . . he put the mitt up for it –

And Dave slammed into him. The ball bounced off somewhere. Dave pulled off the baseball cap he was wearing and slapped Paddy on the chest with it. 'I said it was my ball,' he yelled.

Paddy still hadn't quite forgiven him for the arm-wrestling incident. He smooshed Dave in the face with his mitt, not very gently. 'You are such a divvy, Dave,' he shouted, thoroughly narked. 'That was coming straight down my throat.' He pushed Dave away and stormed off to find the ball.

To cap it all, Tony stalked towards them. 'Why didn't you catch it? It's only bloody rounders.'

Paddy found the ball. 'Well I didn't bloody pick him,' he snarled as he walked past Dave. He tossed the ball to Eddie, who was almost hopping up and down on the mound in impatience.

'Go Mather!' yelled the American CO, Lieutenant Steadman.

Paddy glanced over in that direction. Major Voce was sitting next to him. He looked singularly pissed off. Mather finished his home run, and the Americans exploded into cheers and whistles.

Mather turned to them. He punched the air with both fists. 'Watch and weep, boys,' he jeered. 'Watch and weep.' He ran over to Gallagher and high-fived him.

'That bloke is looking for a punch in the mouth,' Dave said from behind Paddy.

Paddy turned. 'You're pathetic,' he said. He'd had it up to there with Dave, and he couldn't be bothered to pretend. He stalked back to his place.

Gallagher was up next. He came up to the plate to a chorus of cheers and hefted the bat to his shoulder. The Brits cheered Eddie on as he pitched the ball. It whistled past Gallagher's head, straight into Tony's catcher's mitt.

'Strike one,' Sergeant Stein called.

'No way, man,' Gallagher said. 'That was wide, man.'

Stein walked up to him. 'Gallagher, what you have in your hand there is a baseball bat,' he said as if he were talking to a child. 'Now, what you do is you hit the ball with the bat and then you run around the diamond.' He gestured with his hand to show what he meant, then turned away.

'Yes, Sir,' Gallagher said, looking at his feet.

Stein turned back. He jabbed his finger at Gallagher. 'And don't call me "Sir",' he said. 'It's Sergeant Stein.'

'Yes, Sergeant,' Gallagher said.

Oh bad show old chap, Paddy thought. Been pickin' up bad habits from the Brits, have we? The Americans didn't called their non-comms 'Sir'.

'All right,' Stein yelled. He went back to his position. 'Let's play ball. Strike one!'

Paddy was first up when B Platoon had their innings. The Brits – both those waiting on the bench for their turn and those watching the game – roared as he walked up to the plate.

'Go on Paddy,' Dave yelled. He climbed on to the bench and whistled through his fingers. Paddy supposed he was going to have to forgive the prat for his little indiscretions. Tony raised his bat in salute, and just about everyone clapped.

Mather went over to the mound. He chomped on a wodge of gum and gestured to the fielders. 'Come on in, boys. We got a no-hitter,' he yelled.

There was a sudden, uncomfortable silence. Nice one, Mad Mick, Paddy thought: that's the way to make yourself really popular. He raised the bat to his shoulder. Mather wound up for his pitch.

Suddenly Paddy thought of a way to even the score. 'Hold it!' he yelled, motioning Mather to stop. Then he walked forward and used the bat to test the ground, as if he were playing cricket. The rest of the team whooped and cheered, and he saw that even Major Voce was clapping. He did a little two step in acknowledgement, then took up his batting position again.

Mather sneered at him from the mound. Well, Paddy thought – I might have cheered our lot up, but I expect he's going to play hard ball now. He felt a little wave of satisfaction roll over him: if he did well, no-one could say the Yanks had given him an easy time.

Mather pitched. Paddy swung at it and connected

126

hard. The ball flew up into the sky. Paddy didn't see where and didn't care. He just dropped his bat and pelted for first base. And second. His legs pistoned under him. Suddenly he realized the Yank catchers were a damn sight more efficient than he and Dave had been. As he rounded second base, someone threw the ball to Gallagher on third. He forced a little more speed out of himself. Not enough . . . he hurled himself at the base just as Gallagher dropped to his knees with the ball.

'Out!' Gallagher cried.

'I was in, wasn't I?' Paddy said. He got to his feet. 'Here, referee,' he said to Stein, 'I was in, wasn't I?'

'You are out of there,' Stein said, grinning. He jerked his thumb at the bench. The Americans went crazy.

'Catch you later, dude,' Gallagher said.

Fair enough, Paddy thought. He shoved his hands in the pockets of his shorts. 'I never liked the game anyway,' he said as he walked past Stein, who laughed.

An American with a sense of irony, Paddy thought. Well, I never did.


There was a garden party afterwards. Gallagher and Mather stood around the barbecue with Eddie and Paddy. They were all trying to pretend the game had been as friendly as it was supposed to have been, but they weren't succeeding very well. Paddy went off to liberate a couple of beers for him and Mather – Eddie wasn't drinking and Gallagher already had one. As he

127

came back with them, Donna and Joy wandered over. Donna had her arms full with Macaulay; and Joy, of course, was heavily pregnant and trailing little Matthew by the hand. She looked well on it, though – radiant, even – and Tony had been like a dog with two tails over it ever since they got back to Germany.

'Did you win?' she asked.

Paddy just looked at her sourly.

'They put up a good fight,' Gallagher said.

He was being generous. The final score had read nine to zero.

'Hard lines, Paddy,' Eddie said. Paddy grinned at him.

He touched Mather on the arm. 'There you go, big man.' He handed him the beer. He'd briefly considered giving it to Mather with the cap still on, just to see if he'd bite the top off – one of his party tricks, Gallagher had confided – but he'd decided against it. He didn't want to have to clear up the blood.

'Way to go,' Mather said. He slapped Paddy hard on the shoulder, but not so hard it didn't look friendly.

'Listen,' Eddie said. 'We'll have them in the 432s this afternoon.' He picked up a sausage and put it on his plate.

'With you driving?' Paddy said.

'Yes,' Eddie said evenly.

'Listen,' Mather said. 'It could have been worse – it could have been football, and you guys wouldn't even be walking around now –'

'What,' Paddy said. He made a show of not understanding, then said, 'Oh – he means American football, Eddie.' He paused. 'Otherwise known as rugby for wimps.'

He suddenly realized that Gallagher was deep in conversation with Joy. She smiled, and the American reached out and touched her tummy. Joy covered his hand with her own. Naturally, Tony chose to appear at that exact moment. He walked up behind Gallagher.

Paddy got ready to intervene if he had to.

'Qualified, are you?' Tony asked, still from behind the American.

Gallagher only looked a bit embarrassed. 'It's good luck,' he said. 'Uhh . . . Sir.'

Paddy edged a bit closer.

'I wouldn't count on it,' Tony said. He smiled humourlessly.

Luckily, Gallagher realized his danger. 'Ma'am,' he said, and edged away.

Paddy relaxed a bit. 'Tone,' he heard Joy say.

'He was chatting you up,' Tony said firmly.

'He wasn't,' Joy said. 'I'm built like a Chieftain tank.' She put her hands on her tummy. 'Who's going to fancy me like this?'

Tony took a swig of his beer. 'I do,' Tony said, and this time his smile was genuine. He leaned forward and kissed Joy gently but quickly on the lips.

Paddy looked at them. He thought, it would be so nice to have someone here, just for me. And with a sense of bewilderment, he realized he wasn't missing Nancy at all. Someone else would do just as well.

The American and British platoons stood in two lines

in front of their 432s. Paddy caught first Dave's eye and then Eddie's. He knew they were all thinking the same thing: we'll get the bastards now.

Tony stood in front of them holding two red flags crossed in front of him. 'Gentlemen,' he shouted. 'This is straightforward and very simple, as are the rules: the first to finish will be the winner.' He raised the flags above his shoulders. 'Stand by,' he bellowed, and brought them down again.

They turned and raced for the doors of the APC. So did the Yanks, but they were just a bit slower. Eddie had the vehicle in motion before they'd even shut the door, and it rolled out through a haze of red flare smoke. He pulled the hatch down, and started taking orders from Lieutenant Forsythe, who was on the periscope.

Paddy settled himself with his back against the hard metal of the partition. Just in front of them there was a big log. In the next part of the race, they'd run, carrying it suspended on chains, to the finishing line.

But first they had to get through this, and Eddie wasn't taking any prisoners. They jolted and banged around, and he suddenly realized that they were on the stretch of path they'd nicknamed the rollercoaster because of the way it went up and down. It led through a dense patch of woods – if they were leading now, they were going to stay that way unless the Yanks pulled some very sharp tricks.

'We're way ahead,' Forsythe said. A little later he said, 'Driver go right.' He slapped Eddie on the right shoulder to make sure he got the message, as per training.

Eddie cracked the hatch. The APC made one last turn and lost speed. The lads positioned themselves next to the log, and by the time the 432 had slowed down they were ready. Paddy kicked the door open, and they leaped out carrying the log. The Yanks were way behind, still coming round the curve.

But Paddy wasn't taking any chances. 'Left right, left right –' he yelled to force them to pick up the beat. Eddie leaped off the APC and ran ahead of them as they came to the water. They splashed through it, up to their knees in mud. The Yanks were right on their tails, and there was just a chance that they could overtake.

'Get your legs up,' Eddie yelled.

The lads put on a turn of speed. Even so, Paddy noted with some amusement that Brucie was bringing up the rear. Be just the job if our beloved lieutenant makes us lose, he thought. He wondered what Forsythe would do if he had to be helped along.

But they were unstoppable. They charged up the steep slope on the far side of the water. Ahead of them, balloons had been pinned to two trestles, one bearing the Union Jack, the other the Stars and Stripes. Major Voce, Tony and Sergeant Stein were waiting nearby.

They charged their balloon. It banged and the trestles went over. The lads turned and started hollering and cheering as the Americans cleared the water.

Well, that's bowled them over, Paddy thought.

That night in the Naafi, Paddy decided to keep well

clear of the Americans. He still reckoned Mather was trouble on two legs, and he wasn't too chuffed with Dave's behaviour either, so all in all it was easier to find a cosy spot in the corner and wait for those two, plus Eddie and Gallagher, to wind each other up.

It happened sooner rather than later. One minute they were chatting amiably enough. The next Mather was saying, 'No way you would have beaten us if we'd been in an American one-one-three, man.'

'You are a bad loser,' Eddie said. Paddy suddenly realized he had a pint in front of him.

Gawd, he thought. He'd thought Eddie had sworn off after his little binge in Cyprus. It seemed the effects of the hangover had finally worn off.

Mather spread his hands out in front of him. 'If I'd been driving, we would have won.'

That riled Gallagher, who chipped in, 'Are you blaming me?'

That's it, Paddy thought. Bad enough that sooner or later Mather was going to get what was coming to him from one of their lads. If the Americans were arguing between themselves he didn't want to have to explain why he hadn't stopped it to Voce or Brucie or even Tone. He drained his drink, stood up and headed for the door. As he got there he heard Gallagher say, 'You're full of shit, Micky.'

Yep, Paddy thought as he went out into the warm night air, I am definitely better off out of it. He headed to the accommodation block. He sat up reading for a while, then turned in for an early night.

'Paddy!' Someone was shaking him. 'Paddy! Wake up mate.'

Paddy opened one eye. It was night outside, and he could barely make out Eddie's face in the darkness. 'What is it?' he snarled. He tried to turn over and go back to sleep, but Eddie pulled the blanket back. 'All right, all right, Horatio,' he said. 'But this had better be good.'

'It's Joy,' Eddie said. 'She's been hurt –'

'What?' Paddy said; and then again, as it sank in, 'What? You'd better start from the beginning.'

'Well,' Eddie said. 'Gallagher had a go at that Mather, and Mather challenged him to a car race outside –'

'Oh no,' Paddy said. 'I don't want to know –'

Eddie sank down on the edge of the bed. 'Mather raced – no problem. Then Gallagher. I don't know what happened –'

'Wait a minute, Eddie,' Paddy said. 'You aren't telling me you were there –'

Eddie nodded. 'I knew it was stupid. I told Dave we should stop it –'

'Oh not Dave,' Paddy said. 'The stupid bastard. You ought to know better than to let him mess you up, Eddie.'

'Yeah well,' Eddie said. His hand moved convulsively on the white sheet. 'Joy was driving in, and it looked like Gallagher had a blow-out.' He stopped again.

Paddy suddenly realized he was shaking. 'Take it easy, mate,' he said. He patted Eddie on the arm.

133

'Gallagher went into the side of her. She's at the hospital – '

Christ, Paddy thought; but he said, 'Tone?'

'He's with her. There's a chance she might lose the kid, Paddy.' He looked up at Paddy with anguish in his eyes. 'And Dave and me – we've got to see Voce tomorrow. He's already had one go at us, but – ' He took a deep, shuddery breath. 'He says it's in the hands of the RMPs. He says we're guilty by association.' He knotted his hands in front of himself and sat there looking at them for a long moment. 'They can't kick us out, can they, Paddy?'

'I doubt it,' Paddy said. 'If I were you, I'd try to get some sleep.'

He ought to have done the same, but when sleep refused to come he finally gave in, got dressed and went over to the company office. There was just a chance someone might be prepared to tell him something.

To his surprise, the place was ablaze with lights. Paddy looked at his watch. It was far earlier than he had thought – only about eleven thirty. Lieutenant Forsythe was sitting at his desk writing up a report.

'Sir?' Paddy said tentatively.

Forsythe looked up. 'Yes, Corporal?'

'I was wondering if there was any news of Mrs Wilton, Sir – I just heard the news – '

'No news yet, Corporal – they're keeping her in hospital overnight for observation.' Forsythe smiled. It was a smile Paddy knew of old, and it meant either that there was bad news coming or that Forsythe thought he'd got one up on them. Matthew? Paddy

134

wondered. He hoped the little lad was okay. 'But you might be interested to know that Sergeant Wilton has been arrested for beating up Private Gallagher,' Forsythe said. His smile broadened. 'Keep it to yourself, there's a good chap, Garvey. We don't want the whole regiment to know, do we?'

'No, Sir,' Paddy mumbled. He was too shocked even to take it in, let alone talk to anyone about it.

The next day inched by. Tony was released by the RMPs, but he was placed under house arrest and wasn't allowed visitors. Joy had to get complete rest, and it had been decided not to tell her about the trouble until she came home, so they were discouraged from visiting her. Not that Paddy would have had time anyway – he had a special duty: guarding Eddie and Dave while they washed dishes. And damned lucky they were to get off so lightly – as he pointed out to them forcefully and at intervals.

'What are you using, Dave?' Eddie asked. They were up to their elbows in dirty dishwater. 'You're getting through twice as much as me.'

'I know, Eddie,' Dave said. He turned and held a suds-covered hand up to his face, as if posing to camera. 'And these bubbles are so kind to my hands.' He grinned first at Eddie, then at Paddy.

'Oh yes,' Eddie said. He reached forward and tweaked Dave's cheek.

'And look,' Dave continued. He held up a pot. 'No grease.'

Paddy leaned over and said, 'Yes Dave, what is it

135

you're using?' He was thoroughly bored, and knew they were too – but that was part of the punishment. But he also knew that they were using the horseplay to avoid talking about what was on all their minds – Joy and the baby, and whether Tony would be kicked out. Some barracks lawyer somewhere had started a rumour that, because a foreigner was involved, there would not only have to be a court martial, but that a dishonourable discharge would be mandatory. So Paddy wasn't too happy, and he couldn't help blaming himself a bit: he should have known better than to leave Dave in the company of someone like Mad Mick. Eddie was steady enough, but he hadn't been around long enough to know what Dave was really like – and besides, he was easily led.

'Well, Paddy – '

But Paddy grabbed his nose and gave it a good twist. Dave grunted in surprise. 'Shut up and wash up,' Paddy said. 'You're on dirty fatigue, not breakfast television.' He let Dave go.

Eddie turned round and started working again. He sighed. 'Join the British army, keep fit, see the world and wash up,' he said.

'Just take your punishment like a man, Nelson,' Paddy said.

Just then, Mather and Gallagher came in. Gallagher had a cut under one eye and a split lip, but he didn't look as bad as Paddy had expected. 'Hi,' he said softly. 'We're leaving today.' He sounded thoroughly pissed off, which was entirely understandable, Paddy reckoned. 'The exchange's been cut short. We just wanted to . . .' he let his voice trail off. By all accounts he'd been trying to apologize when Tony laid into him. Perhaps he thought Paddy and the others would do the same.

'Sergeant Wilton's got a kid, right?' Mather cut in. He laid a baseball bat, mitt and ball down on one side. 'Can you just see that he gets these?'

They didn't say another word. Gallagher still looked as if he wanted to say something, but he never did find the words. Mather clapped him on the shoulder, and they left.

'Bang goes our trip to the US of A,' Eddie muttered at their retreating backs.

'Grow up, Nelson,' Paddy said. Dave looked at him. 'Scrub,' Paddy finished.

Tony only had one piece of luck – they managed to fit his court martial in the next week, mostly because of the effect on Joy and the baby. He wasn't allowed to see anyone, but Donna visited Joy and came back saying she was taking it badly.

That hardly came as a shock, Paddy thought – everyone else was, too. Some people you expected to screw up – it had been no surprise to him, for example, to come back from his Platoon Sergeant's Battle Course and find that Dave had got sucked into a bet Brucie had taken on to pass one of the men off as an officer. But Tony was different – he lived for the army. He had a perfect record, and everyone had always assumed he'd make it to CSM and beyond. He cared about his mates of course, but that was different. And then there was Joy, on whom he doted.

He'd had one fling with a girl in New Zealand, and come close to losing her. Since then, he'd been as much the model husband as he was the model sergeant.

The only thing that surprised Paddy was that Tony had left Gallagher in a state fit to walk away.

After a week dominated by rumour and speculation, and in which the only thing they had to take their minds off it was getting ready to march out to England, the day of the court martial finally arrived. There was nothing they could do for Tony – he had Voce to defend him, which gave Paddy some hope – and as Donna said, it was Joy who really needed their support.

So they all went with her to wait in the hall outside the court. Joy looked as if she'd hardly slept. Her skin was ashen, and her long dark hair was in a straggly ponytail. Donna sat next to her, looking demure – for Donna – in a tiny black skirt suit. Eddie and Paddy sat opposite, perching on the uncomfortable plastic chairs that were all that had been provided. Paddy turned his beret round and round in his hands. When he comes out, he thought, Tony might not be allowed to wear this. They could chuck him out. They could send him to Colchester for a term in the slammer. They could bust him back to fusilier, and if they do that they'll move him out of B Company for sure, even if they let him stay in the King's Own. That might be the worst of all.

Or they could even combine the three.

'It's the big day,' Dave said, in blatant disregard of the Silence sign. He was leaning against the wall. No-one answered him. What the bloody hell could you say, when he made it sound like a wedding or something? He tossed his beret up so it flipped over. 'Well it is!' he said defensively. He started to pace up and down. Typical bloody Tucker, Paddy thought. If you'd told him to patrol, he'd have found a wall to skulk behind.

'Don't worry, Dave,' Joy said. 'I can't worry any more than I am doing.' That was typical of Joy. Paddy knew she drove Donna and the other wives mad – he remembered Nancy complaining about her sometimes – because she was always fretting, and she got completely neurotic when anything needed doing. But she was also kind-hearted to a fault, and he'd told Dave over and over again that she probably didn't blame him and Eddie for what had happened – in fact, Joy being Joy, she'd probably found a way not to blame Gallagher, too.

'Are you sure you don't want to go in there, Joy?' Paddy asked.

'I'd just make a fool of myself,' she whispered. Her eyes were red from crying, and the floral maternity dress and white cardigan she was wearing made her seem to disappear against the cream walls.

Paddy leaned back in his chair. There wasn't anything to say, really.

That didn't stop Eddie trying. He turned to Paddy. 'Don't you think . . . under the circumstances . . .' he let his voice trail off.

Under the circumstances, some people in the company thought they ought to be pinning a medal on Tony. But he could hardly say that; and besides, he didn't want to give Joy any false hope at all. 'Let's just wait and see what happens, shall we?'

They lapsed into silence. It was so nearly me, Paddy thought. I so nearly put my mates through this . . . it had been back when Nancy had left him. He'd gone off the rails a bit – tried to stop CSM Stubbs' daughter going off with an older man. She'd slapped his face for his trouble, and the thought that he couldn't do anything right – not for Nancy, not for her – had made him crack. When he'd got back to the base, he'd taken an APC for a spin. Only Tony had stopped him, made him see sense. And then Sarah had told her parents he'd assaulted her.

He'd ended up in the slammer. The days he'd spent there had blurred into one terrible memory that could still make his stomach knot. He could have ended up with nothing – no career and certainly no Nancy. Only luck had saved him. First Sarah Stubbs had come clean at the last minute. And then there'd been a fire in the crèche, right by where they'd put him to work; backhanded luck, that – the fire could have cost lives. As it was, he'd managed to save a baby's life, and that had persuaded the then Captain Voce to go easy on him.

Tony wouldn't have any such luck. All he'd have was his impeccable record and the hope that the president of the court and the other judges would be able to understand, if not excuse, what he'd done.

'It's going to be some party tonight, isn't it?' Eddie whispered when the silence had stretched on so long it was unbearable. 'Smashing farewell to Germany.'

'You packed?' Paddy asked by way of a reply.

'Just about,' Eddie said.

There was another long, painful pause. 'What about you, Joy?' Paddy asked, trying to sound cheerful. 'You all packed up and everything?'

Joy didn't answer, just smiled and nodded. Paddy got the feeling that if she tried to speak she might have cried instead. Dave was standing facing the wall. He turned and stared mournfully at her.

Paddy said, 'Yeah, I bet you can't wait to get out of this dump, hey?' As soon as he'd said it, he wished he could take the words back.

Dave turned round. 'And you think I'm tactless,' he said to Joy.

Donna smiled ruefully and patted Joy's hand, but Joy just seemed to grow more despondent.

A little while later, Eddie went and got everyone cups of tea from the Naafi. They drank them in silence, and Paddy took the cups back. When he returned, it struck him that there was no telling how long they'd been sitting there – it could have been minutes or hours, or conceivably days.

Dave was pacing again, but this time he was measuring his steps as if he were marching. His boots clumped on the hard floor. Paddy sat down as Donna said, 'Give over, Dave. You're not on guard duty now.'

Dave turned. He glared at Donna, and Paddy suddenly remembered that he'd said they were having a

141

bad time. But then Joy looked up, and Dave somehow managed to turn the glare into a rueful little smile.

'I just hope they don't kick him out,' Joy said suddenly to Donna. 'He couldn't stand that. He lives for the army.' He lives for you, Paddy thought; whatever Joy believed, he knew that given the choice, Tony would willingly have given up the army to keep her safe with him. He'd said as much when he'd thought she was starting an affair with her aikido instructor. 'Please don't let them kick him out,' she said. She took a long, ragged breath, and then looked at her hands again.

Dave and Paddy locked gazes. They both knew it was a possibility. Don't you say a word, Dave Tucker, Paddy thought. Dave had already been this route once before, and ended up in Colchester Military Prison with no Donna waiting for him when he came out — he above all should know how rough it was for Joy.

And then, finally, the door opened.

Paddy was on his feet instantly. He got to the door before Tony even came out. The others all clustered around, too. Tony marched to the door. He was smart in his dress uniform, but ashen-faced and Paddy would have sworn he was shaking.

'So is it good or bad, Sarge?' he asked.

Tony looked at him grimly as he walked down the steps into the hall. 'Bad,' he said dully. 'Very bad.' Then he grinned. 'And that's Corporal to you, Ugly.'

It took a second for it to register. Then Paddy

realized that all they'd done was take one of Tony's stripes away. It was the mildest of possible punishments – far milder than anyone had expected. 'Well done, mate,' he said, but by that time Tony was hugging Joy, who had tears streaming down her face.

Major Voce came down the steps. He was barely managing to suppress a grin.

'Well done, Sir,' Paddy said. Voce smiled at him.

Later that afternoon, Paddy was ordered in to see Major Voce. From the way CSM Stubbs told him about it, he didn't think it was trouble, and in any case he hadn't done anything he knew of that would warrant Major Voce's involvement.

That left only one thing it could be. But he refused even to consider that.

He knocked on the door, waited for permission to enter, and went inside. Major Voce was standing by his wall planner. He turned to Paddy, who shut the door and saluted. 'You wanted to see me, Sir,' he said.

'Yes, Garvey,' the Major said. 'Sit down.' He gestured at an empty space in front of his desk.

Paddy grabbed a chair from the far wall and placed it in front of the desk. He sat down and took his beret off. Now he was sure he'd been right about the purpose of this interview. He licked his lips. Sitting down in front of an officer instead of standing to attention made him nervous. He smoothed his hair back anxiously.

'Well,' Major Voce said. 'As you know there's a

vacancy for a platoon sergeant in B Company.' So I was right, Paddy thought. He'd hoped he was wrong. This wasn't a decision he wanted to make. 'How do you feel about that?'

Confused, Paddy thought. He'd worked so hard for this – right from the start, and then especially when he'd had to make up lost ground from all the mistakes he made after Nancy left him. 'Platoon sergeant,' he said, to buy himself some thinking time. There was always the chance that Tony was being moved out of B Company, even though he'd been told he could stay in the King's Own.

'I know it's difficult with Wilton being busted down to corporal, but you have to think about the next step up,' Voce said. 'And it's felt that you're the best man for the job.'

Paddy knew he was right; but he'd always assumed that Tony would be promoted ahead of him at best; or that at worst, he'd have to move to another platoon when he got promoted himself. 'Tony Wilton's a good mate of mine, Sir,' he said. He wondered what Voce would say if he turned the promotion down. One thing was certain – it would be a long time before he made Paddy another offer.

'I know,' Voce said. He smiled encouragingly. 'That's why I want you to be his sergeant.'

'So . . . you're keeping him in the company,' Paddy said, again buying himself time.

'He's been a bloody fool,' the major said, 'but I can't afford to lose a man of that experience.' Well, that was one relief, Paddy thought. 'I want to keep an eye on him, get him back on his feet – and that's where you can help.' He grinned. 'I just need to convince the CO. Anyway, I need an answer in the morning.' He paused. 'And it had better be yes. On your way.'

Paddy put his beret on, got up, replaced the chair, saluted and left, almost without noticing what he was doing. Sergeant Paddy Garvey, he thought. Sergeant Garvey. *Sergeant* Garvey. But each time he thought it, he saw Tony looking at him, and it took the edge off it.

I could ask him what I should do, he thought; but he knew that Tony would never hold him back. So why, when he saw Tony's face in his mind, did he look so betrayed?

Eddie was right, Paddy decided. It wasn't much of a leaving party. Paddy sat with him and Dave and Donna in the Naafi, but he could hardly bear to look at them. He hadn't told them about his possible promotion – how could he, when they would want to celebrate it, yet it meant stabbing Tony in the back? Whatever Voce said about helping him. So he just sat nursing a pint and not saying very much.

'Do you think they'll come?' Donna asked.

'Who?' Dave asked, though he must have known the answer.

'Joy and Tony,' Donna said. She looked round at the bar. 'It's a bit of a comedown, isn't it, after the refineries of the sergeants' mess?'

Dave drained his glass. 'I think you mean refinements, Donna,' he said. He smiled, but the sarcasm was clear. They never seemed to have big rows any more; they just spent all their time sniping at each other, and that worried Paddy much more.

'I know what I mean,' Donna said. She seemed hurt, whereas before she would have snapped back. Something is definitely going on with those two, Paddy thought. Knowing them, it would probably be best to keep well clear, unless one of them wanted to talk about it.

'Take a bit of neck, that's for sure,' Eddie said, back to the previous topic. Evidently he'd figured it out, too.

'You're very quiet, Paddy,' Dave said.

Here we go, Paddy thought. He took a long drink of lager while he tried to think of an excuse, but since he couldn't, he just said, 'Am I?'

'Top vibe,' Donna said, sounding thoroughly pissed off.

'Anyway, proud man, our Anthony,' Dave said. 'Wouldn't want to come in here and listen to this lot mouthing off.'

The door opened. Wrong again, Tucker, Paddy thought. Tony walked into the room, with Joy but minus his moustache. The pair of them looked round almost shyly.

Paddy was on his feet in an instant. He started to clap, and then everyone else joined in. There was a chorus of warwhoops and whistles. 'Go Tony!' someone shouted from the back of the room.

Paddy went up to Tony. 'Don't let the bastards grind you down, hey Tone?' he said. He shook his friend's hand.

'Never,' Tony said. 'I've heard they're looking for a new sergeant.' He paused. Paddy thought, if he asked me not to do it, I'll go with that. But Tony went on, 'You've got my vote.'

Paddy felt his eyes go wide as the tension left him. He wondered if Tony had noticed, and then decided it didn't matter. I ought to say something, he thought; but there weren't enough words in the world, so he just smiled.

The music changed, and 'You'll Never Walk Alone' began to play. Tony took his jacket off, and gave it to Paddy. He turned to Joy and took her hand. Together they went out onto the dance floor, to a renewed barrage of claps and cheers. Dave whistled, but all Paddy could do was watch them as they moved across the floor. He'll be all right, he thought. He may have lost his third stripe, but he's got what he needs most.

The thought flashed through Paddy's mind that though he had the extra stripe, he didn't have the thing that he needed most. Time to move on, he told himself firmly. Time to move on.

# Chapter 6

It was strange to be back in Britain, and stranger still to be in the sergeants' mess. Paddy had asked Tony a lot of questions about it, but the most he'd got out of him was one warning not to run up a huge mess bill, and another to make sure he kept his mess kit clean at all times.

Tony hadn't said anything about an initiation ceremony.

It hadn't occurred to Paddy that senior NCOs would arse around just as much as the men did, but here they were cheering him on as he walked the length of the mirror-polished dining table. He had one arm behind his back. The other was stretched out in front of him, and there was a glass of claret balanced on the back of his hand, and he was supposed to serve it to the regimental sergeant major. At least they weren't pounding the table, he thought.

He'd made it so far, but his arm was beginning to ache. He picked his way round a heavy silver candlestick. That was fairly easy, but then he had to turn. For one awful second he thought he felt his heel slide from under him, but he managed to stop it. He swallowed. Down, now, he thought. He bent at the knees. The glass wobbled alarmingly, and he had a vision of half the senior NCOs in the regiment sending him their cleaning bills. Just a little more . . . a little more, and then the RSM took the glass.

There was a lot of table pounding then, and he found himself being dragged off the table and taken to the bar. So this is how they get those huge mess bills, he thought, as he bought a full round.

'Sar'nt Garvey!' CSM Stubbs said, raising his pint. The others cheered – even if he was only an acting sergeant, and would be for the several months until his rank was confirmed.

Paddy chinked glasses with Stubbs. 'Sar'nt Garvey,' he said, hoping to high heaven he'd prove up to it.

Paddy marched the platoon out. He still wasn't really at ease, it seemed strange not to be in the ranks, and wearing the Number 1 dress uniform, with its peaked cap rather than a beret and hackle – to say nothing of the weight of the third stripe on his arm – just added to the feeling of unfamiliarity.

He called them to a halt. 'Left turn,' he yelled, and they turned to face him.

CSM Stubbs approached them from the other side of the parade ground, accompanied by a fusilier Paddy didn't recognize.

'Sar'nt Garvey – new man for the platoon,' CSM Stubbs said. 'Fusilier Farrell.' He turned and left.

'All right, lads,' Paddy said. He could see that Tony and Dave were excited about something, but he decided to ignore it. 'We have a new specimen. Goes by the name of Fusilier Farrell. I trust you will make him at home.' He realized he knew exactly what to do next, and that pleased him: the first few times he'd taken drill, he'd been certain he would cock it up. 'Centre rank, fill your left,' he shouted. The middle row of men crabbed sideways, leaving a space behind Dave. 'Tucker dress back,' Paddy shouted. Dave took two paces back, leaving a gap next to Tony, as Paddy had planned – he wanted the new lad to have a good example to follow. 'Go on in, son,' he said, and it was only then that it occurred to him that this Farrell was approximately his own age – making him, like Eddie, a late starter.

As Farrell took his place, he murmured something – either to Tony or Dave, Paddy wasn't sure. He made his mind up to find out what was going on once drill finished.


A little later, the platoon did weapons drill. It was necessary because they were going to be on show, as they did ceremonial duty outside Windsor Castle.

Paddy slow marched them down the parade ground. They carried their rifles at the slope. 'Left,' he yelled. Pause. 'Right.' Pause. 'Left.' They weren't bad, considering what most of them thought of ceremonial duties. It was just as well. CSM Stubbs was pacing them, and Paddy desperately didn't want to be embarrassed in front of him.

'Platoon. Halt,' he said, projecting his voice across the parade ground without actually shouting. The platoon halted as one, with a single satisfying slam of boots against the tarmac. 'Present arms,' Paddy called.

The men brought their rifles round in front of them in perfect unison – all but the new boy, Farrell, who dropped his. It clattered to the ground.

'Oops a daisy.' Tucker's voice rang out clear as a bell across the square.

At least Farrell had the wit not to try and pick his rifle up. Paddy finished the drill, then went over to him. By that time, CSM Stubbs had taken up a position at the front of the platoon.

Paddy confronted Farrell. Dave, standing next to him, grinned. Paddy simply pulled the corners of his mouth down with his fingers. 'Don't embarrass me in front of the Drill Sergeant, there's a good lad,' he said to Farrell. 'Now, let's see if you can get it right this time.' He raised his voice. 'Pick up your rifle and take two places forward.'

Farrell did so. He came to attention, looking vaguely embarrassed.

'Present arms,' Paddy shouted for him alone. Farrell brought the weapon round in front of him. Paddy corrected its tilt slightly. 'Strike the rifle, bend the knee,' he roared. 'Slope arms.' Farrell got the weapon up on his shoulder. Paddy looked at him critically. 'We're getting there,' he said, without any noticeable sign of approval entering his voice. 'Fall back in.'

Farrell walked backwards into his place. 'He's new isn't he – potato nose?' Paddy heard him mutter to Tony. He chose to ignore it, and waited for Tony to put the man down instead.

151

But all Tony said was, 'Yeah.'

Well, Paddy thought, I knew taking his rank wasn't going to be easy, even if he did tell me to go for it.

Paddy kept out of the way of the others while he was off duty for the next couple of days. Tony seemed to need more time to adjust to his reduced rank, and Dave was mooching around – Paddy suspected he and Donna were still having a bad time, but he wouldn't say. It was easy enough – Paddy just stuck to the sergeants' mess instead of going to the bar in the Naafi. After all, it was only what was expected of him anyway.

He found out third-hand that Joe Farrell had been in the French Foreign Legion before he joined the King's Own, and that despite being a bit of a Jack the Lad, he had a girlfriend called Colette. She was quite the career woman – the manager of a travel agent's in Windsor – and though Farrell wanted to marry her, she kept turning him down. Paddy didn't really care – he reckoned Farrell was trouble in the making – but he'd taken up with Tony and Dave, so undoubtedly he was going to have to rub along with him eventually.

But work was another matter entirely, and before very long their first public duty came around. Paddy marched them out behind the pipe and drum band, acutely aware that they were being watched not only by a large crowd of tourists – how could he forget, when every few seconds a camera went off – but also by the wives.

Everything was fine, until Dave got out of step. Then he dropped his rifle and bumped into the man behind him, and within seconds Paddy had a shambles on his hands.

'Pick that bloody rifle up,' CSM Stubbs screamed.

Sod it, Dave, Paddy thought. You would cock it up. But later Eddie told him that Farrell had screwed Dave up by making him think he was out of step — and that Tony had had a short, sharp word with him about it.

Nice one, Tony, Paddy thought. But he still didn't want to talk to him.

A few days after that, CSM Stubbs had an announcement for part of the platoon. He faced them on the parade ground. Paddy didn't know what it was all about, except that he'd been told to find ten men to take part in an assault course. He'd included Farrell in order to bring him on a bit; and Tony, because he needed the boost. Eddie was a natural, and Tucker had somehow slid in as well — he might mess things up, but on the rare occasions when he didn't, he did a good job — and no-one had ever questioned his fitness.

'Right. You have been volunteered for the honour of representing B Company in a competition that will form the highlight of the Regiment's D-Day commemorative celebrations. Not only will you win that competition, you will win it in style . . . 1940s style.' He turned towards the accommodation block and yelled. 'Tucker! Doubling!'

153

Tucker appeared and trotted over. He looked like something out of 'Dad's Army', with his baggy combat trousers and brimmed helmet. The Lee Enfield rifle he was carrying was a museum piece too.

Most of the lads fell about laughing. Only Tony barely cracked a smile; and, Paddy realized, Dave looked more distracted than embarrassed.

Things are going on with those two, he thought, and it's not all down to that Scouser Farrell. He made up his mind all over again to find out what was up.

He didn't have long to wait. Joy phoned him that afternoon in a real state. He arranged to meet her, and was surprised when she insisted he meet her in a café miles from the married quarters. She looked rough – not as bad as when Tony was court martialled, but not that far off, either. He got her a mug of tea and they sat at the formica-topped table while she told him the bad news; she'd been trying to sell the car, it had been stolen, and she didn't dare tell Tony.

'But you've told the police?' he asked. He sipped his tea. It was too weak and not sweet enough.

'I've given them the description – I mean, I was with him for half an hour.' She rested her chin on her hands. 'They will catch him, won't they?' Then she added quickly, 'I thought Joe Farrell might hear something – through his cabbing.' The platoon's newest recruit had somehow managed to wangle permission to work on the side. Paddy didn't approve, but the permission was genuine enough so he'd just kept quiet about it.

For a split second he considered saying something reassuring. But it would only make it worse in the end. He took her hand in both of his. 'Listen, Joy,' he said. 'The car's probably already been resprayed by now. Tomorrow it'll be on some garage forecourt a hundred miles from here.' Joy's eyes glistened. This isn't just about the car, Paddy thought – it can't be or she wouldn't be worried about telling him. He stroked her hand.

'What am I going to tell Tone?' Joy sounded near panic.

It couldn't be that bad, Paddy thought. She must know that Tony would have walked through fire for her. 'Well, you're just going to have to tell him, aren't you?' he said at last. 'He'll be pissed off, but – '

'I can't,' Joy wailed, and now she was crying. Tears glistened on her cheeks. 'I threatened to leave him yesterday – '

'What?' Paddy exclaimed. It explained Tony's mood during drill, if nothing else. 'Why?'

'He lost the money I'd put by for decorating Matthew's room,' Joy said. They'd be finding things tight now Tony was only on a corporal's pay. It couldn't help, anyway, Paddy thought. 'Gambling,' Joy said bitterly. 'I made him promise, after that time in Hong Kong.' She wiped at her eyes with the heel of her hand. 'I think he's cracking up. It's not just that. He's drinking. And now that you're . . .' she stumbled to a halt.

'That I've taken his rank,' Paddy helped her out. 'I know.'

155

'He doesn't blame you,' Joy said quickly. 'I know he doesn't. But he isn't handling it very well. And now he's lost his precious car . . . I just don't know what to do.'

'But Joy, he's going to notice – I mean, it's his car,' Paddy said. 'He's going to see it's gone and – '

'No,' Joy cut him off. 'I left a note saying I'd gone to stay at my cousin's for a couple of days, so he'll think I've got the car – '

Paddy stared through the net curtains at the road outside. She made it sound very logical, but Paddy reckoned that it was no wonder Tony was upset – he probably thought she'd gone off while she tried to decide whether or not to leave him. 'But you're still going to have to talk about it, aren't you?' he said, tentatively.

'I don't know how to talk to him any more, Paddy,' Joy said.

It sounded so familiar – exactly the way he'd felt when Nancy left him. As if all the words disappeared into the air the moment you said them, and never reached the other person's ears at all.

'Do you want me to try?' he asked, thinking, don't say yes. Don't say yes. Please, don't say yes.

But Joy nodded. Paddy thought, that's it then. I'm a dead man.

The first chance Paddy got was at the D-Day celebrations. The site had been decked out in 40s style, and though the men were wearing their regular dress uniforms – complete with beret and hackle, to Paddy's great relief – the women were all in costume, from land girls with their hair shoved up under turbans, to city sophisticates in long skirts and high heels. The place was also awash with veterans who were there to relive their pasts, and families with young kids who gawped as much at anyone in a uniform as at the decommissioned bren gun emplacements and ancient tanks that dotted the place. It would have been a fun day, if only the promise he'd made Joy weren't making a knot of tension in Paddy's belly.

He spotted Tony and went over to him. 'Listen, mate,' he said. 'I was wondering if I could have a word.'

'What about?' Tony asked. He didn't sound happy.

Paddy took a deep breath. 'You and Joy.'

Tony's face went blank. His hands knotted into fists. 'None of your business,' he said and walked away. As Paddy watched, he walked over to Joy, who was talking to Fusilier Knox's girlfriend, while simultaneously doing a good impersonation of a barrage balloon in a huge pair of dungarees and pulled her away.

Paddy realized that Dave had been watching Donna from a distance. He had a wistful look on his face. Like Joy, Donna was wearing a turban and dungarees, but she managed to make them look as sexy as the mini skirts and stilettoes she usually favoured.

Dave came up to him. 'Paddy, you got a minute?' he asked.

But Paddy had had a bellyful of other people's marital problems. 'No, mate,' he said. 'I'm busy.'

157

He regretted that later, when Dave didn't turn up in time to change into costume for the assault-course race. Some of the veterans were in the tent with them, helping them wear the uniforms correctly.

'I'd be more comfortable in a hair shirt,' Joe Farrell complained.

'Don't make me laugh, laddie,' one of the veterans said to a chorus of approval from his friends, and gave Joe's shirt a vicious tug.

'Hang about, has anyone seen Dave?' Paddy asked when he finally realized Tucker wasn't there.

Too late. CSM Stubbs walked in. 'All ready, lads?'

'I'm afraid not, Sergeant Major,' Paddy said uncomfortably. 'We appear to be one man down.'

Stubbs smiled without humour. 'Let me guess.' He ducked back through the tent flap.

Dave eventually arrived with minutes to spare, trailing a veteran of his very own. He started to get changed, but before he'd got far, CSM Stubbs came charging in after him.

'Do you want to send me to an early grave?' he demanded.

Tucker held up his 1940s combat trousers in front of him, like a shield. 'Not really, Sir,' he said.

CSM Stubbs opened his mouth to start the bollocking Dave so richly deserved, but at that moment the veteran Dave had brought with him cut in. 'It was my fault, I'm afraid,' he said. 'We got talking.' Paddy could just imagine – the old boy's chest was covered in medals.

Stubbs turned. His expression changed rapidly. 'It's Mr Knight, isn't it?'

'Yes,' the old man said softly.

Stubbs thrust a hand at him. 'It's a privilege to meet you, Sir,' he said. 'But where's your Military Medal?'

The old man looked abashed. He reached in his pocket and brought out yet another medal. He held it out for Stubbs to see. 'Let's just say there wasn't room for it,' he said, smiling.

Bloody hell, Paddy thought. The Military Medal was almost as high as decorations went.

Stubbs smiled at the old man in evident admiration – but only for a couple of seconds. Then he turned back to Dave. 'Don't just stand there gawping, man,' he barked. Dave fumbled at his uniform. Stubbs spoke to the room as a whole. 'You lot – get yourselves down to the start line NOW!'

Mr Knight had a surprise in store for them. 'I'd like to have a go,' he said to Stubbs' retreating back, but the CSM didn't hear.

'Pardon?' Paddy said, not quite believing what he'd heard.

'I would,' the old man insisted.

Paddy thought about it for a few seconds, and decided there were times when there were more important things than winning. 'I suppose we could –'

'I'll stand down,' Joe said.

'No, you're okay,' Paddy said. He wanted to bring Joe into the platoon a bit more. He looked around for someone else. Still stinging a bit from the earlier conversation, he said, 'Tony – get your kit off and give it to Mr Knight.' Tony looked mortified.

'Oh no,' Mr Knight said. 'No.'

'It'll be his pleasure, I'm sure, Sir,' Paddy said. He glared at Tony, who didn't move. 'Ah – that's an order, Corporal,' he added.

Tony managed a thin smile.

Paddy almost regretted his gesture a bit later, during the race itself. The rest of his team had done well, first crawling under barbed wire through billowing flare smoke, then throwing a log across a ditch and running across it, past a couple of burning tyres, to the cheers and whistles of the crowd. But the old man had delayed them at every point, and Paddy realized he desperately wanted to win.

'Give him a hand,' he yelled to Dave. 'Come on Jack – any time this week'll do.'

The old man staggered across the bridge and up to the gun emplacement. There was only the casualty evacuation to see to now, and they'd be home and dry. But the C Company team was way ahead of them – they were already breaking the stretchers out of their ambulance.

'Charlie Fire Team – two stretchers from the ambulance!' Paddy shouted. 'Move!'

Farrell and the others moved off, but they had too much to make up – Paddy couldn't see how they could do it. He motioned to the rest of the team, and they ran up to the casualties – mansized, floppy dolls – ready to evacuate them.

'Never mind the stretchers – go for a fireman's lift, Sergeant,' Jack said.

Paddy blinked. It was so obvious it was brilliant –

nothing in the instructions Paddy had been given said they had to use stretchers. 'Thank you,' he muttered to Jack. He thrust his rifle into the old man's hands. 'Come on,' he said. He heaved one of the dolls over his shoulder, while Knox took the second and Dave and Jack followed with the rifles.

They trotted up to the ambulance, and got aboard. Jack drove them over the finish line while the C Company team was still putting its casualties on the stretchers.

A bit later, they lined up so CSM Stubbs and Isobel Jennings, the colonel's wife, could congratulate them. Jack Knight looked like a new man.

While they were still standing there, Tony came running up. Joy had gone into labour. Paddy organized an ambulance. Tony climbed aboard.

'You all right, mate?' Paddy asked up at him from the ground.

'I am now,' Tony said. 'Did you know the car had been stolen? She was too scared to tell me.' Paddy grinned. 'I thought she was leaving me ... Christ, I know I haven't been easy to live with since –'

'You'll do better,' Paddy said, and knew it was true. He shut the door of the ambulance on his friend, and watched as it rolled out.

They'd be okay, he decided. Tony knew what was important.

# Chapter 7

A couple of days later, Paddy walked into the sergeants' mess. It was gone ten and the place was closed up, but Paddy had expected that – he'd known in advance it would be a late night. He had been out with Tony and the others, wetting the baby's head – Joy had given birth to a bouncing baby girl they had decided to call Lauren – and Eddie had introduced them all to his new girlfriend, Melanie. Not that he seemed half so keen on her as she obviously was on him.

Paddy wasn't drunk – well not very – but he was hungry. That was okay, though, because he'd arranged with the cooks to leave him a sandwich. There was a silver dome sitting on a trolley near the bar. That'll be it, he thought happily. He lifted the lid. A scrap of lettuce looked up at him. He pulled a face at it, wondering which other bugger had got there first.

A sound behind him made him turn. A small, short-haired woman was locking up the dining room. ''Scuse me,' Paddy called. He walked in her direction, carrying the plate.

She turned and came towards him.

'Hiya,' he said. She had an elfin face, all high

cheekbones and wide eyes, but a well-toned body – a bit like Bjork on steroids, Paddy thought. 'I told the mess staff I was going to miss supper, yeah?' he said. 'They said they'd leave some sarnies out for me.' He held the plate out.

'So?' she said without any visible sign of interest.

'So this,' Paddy said, looking mournfully at the plate.

'Looks like someone got there first,' she said, grinning. Dimples appeared either side of her mouth.

'I worked that out for myself,' Paddy said, and regretted it immediately. What was required here was obviously an application of the famous Garvey charm.

'And what am I supposed to do about it?' The woman glared up at him – she barely came up to his chest.

Paddy grinned lopsidedly, which generally had the desired effect on women. 'You couldn't knock us up a little something, could you?'

She laughed in mock astonishment. 'The kitchen's closed,' she said.

'I'm starving,' Paddy protested. 'I've only had a packet of crisps – I need more than that.'

'Ooh you poor thing. My heart bleeds.' She had a distinct cockney accent. 'Still,' she said, grinning wickedly. 'Only eight hours till breakfast. Goodnight.'

She turned and left. 'Goodnight,' Paddy said. He munched dispiritedly on his lettuce leaf.

As part of community relations, the company had

laid on a five-a-side charity football match with the locals, to raise money for the local youth club. That was to take place on the Sunday, so of course Brucie had arranged extra training on Saturday afternoon. The team, selected from all ranks, assembled in the gym. It was a good work out, but about half way through the door swung open and Lieutenant Forsythe came in. He was followed in by a small, tough-looking woman in a leotard.

Knox wolf-whistled from the back of the gym.

'Thank you, Fusilier,' Brucie said.

Paddy could only stare – it was the woman he'd met the night before. She looked even better in a leotard than she had in jeans. She grinned at him as she put the ghetto-blaster she was carrying down on the floor.

'All right, gentlemen. This is Sergeant Hawkins.' Brucie gestured to the woman.

'Morning, Sergeant Garvey,' she said breezily.

That earned Paddy a quizzical glance from Tony. 'Morning, Sergeant Hawkins,' he managed.

'Sergeant Hawkins is a bit of a star, not only with steak and kidney pie, but with training – circuit work,' Brucie said. Sergeant Hawkins looked up at him as if she thought he was a bit of a prat. Score one for the lady in the leotard, Paddy thought. 'She's more than capable of putting you bunch through your paces, and I said you'd like to have a go,' Brucie finished, as if he'd done them a massive favour.

Well, Paddy thought, this isn't going to be too much of a problem. He looked at Tony. 'Yes, Sir,' they both said. A certain amount of foot shuffling and coughing behind them indicated what the men thought about it. I'll have words with the first bloke who takes the piss out of her, Paddy decided. It was hardly her fault if Brucie had set her up — it was probably another one of his little bets.

'Over to you, Sergeant Hawkins,' Forsythe said and started towards the door.

'Are you not joining in, sir?' Hawkins asked.

Brucie waved his clipboard at her. ''Fraid I can't — paperwork. Sorry.' He left.

Sergeant Hawkins turned the music on. 'Right,' she said. 'Here we go.'

She started into an aerobics routine. It was simple enough at first — elbow to opposite knee and reverse. Step to the side, to the side. Reverse and repeat . . . Paddy found he had to count to keep the rhythm, but that was hard because he was suddenly aware of the bunch of blokes who'd gathered to watch from the gallery.

'Use your breathing,' Hawkins said. 'And step and two and three and back and two and three and down — ' she bobbed down, and clicked her fingers. Paddy couldn't match her. The damned woman was built out of springs, he reckoned. He couldn't take his eyes off her. Someone on the gallery jeered. He waved them away, but now they were supposed to be moving left only he was still on the way up. He tried the move just as the others went right —

'Right is the opposite of left, Sar'nt Garvey,' Hawkins called, to Paddy's chagrin.

He managed to get back in step.

And then she upped the pace.

Afterwards, he had to admit it had been a damned good workout. As he left the gym, he heard Eddie say to her, 'That was great – thanks Sarge.'

Paddy wished he'd thought to say it. He hurried to catch up with her. 'Not as easy as you thought, Sergeant Garvey?' she asked innocently.

He ignored it. 'Listen, I am really sorry about last night,' he said. 'I was a bit drunk and I made a prat of myself.' As a chat-up line, it lacked a certain something, but it was better than nothing.

Or maybe not. 'You do it very well,' she said. Her eyes sparkled.

'Thank you,' Paddy said.

Hawkins moved off. He matched her pace. 'Listen, how about a chance to make it up?' he asked.

She looked at him slyly. 'Sorry, Sergeant. I don't date soldiers.'

'Neither do I,' Paddy said. He suddenly realized that there were just a few chestnut highlights in her dark hair. 'Anyway, it's not a date – it's just I thought maybe you could come along to the footie on Sunday. Give us a bit of support.' It would be so nice to know there was someone watching specially for him, he thought. He glanced at her, suddenly aware that sweat was pouring off him, while she looked relatively cool and calm. But she was definitely thinking about it. He went for the kill. 'Afterwards, we could go for a pizza or something – if you like.' He tried to make it sound as if it made no odds at all to him.

166

Hawkins stopped walking. She grinned, that impish grin he'd already come to expect. 'I'll tell you what,' she said slowly. 'I'll do you a deal. I'll come and watch you play football if you come to my step aerobics class tomorrow morning.'

Oh no, Paddy thought. It wasn't the thought of making a fool of himself in front of a room full of women, though that was on the cards. It was the fact that for the first time in ages he already had plans for a Saturday morning. 'I'm sorry – ' he started.

'Do you good,' Hawkins said. Paddy swallowed. 'But only if your ego can stand it.'

'No!' Paddy said quickly. 'No, I would – it's just that I've already fixed to go down the river with my brother and his kid.' She didn't believe him. 'I'm hiring a skiff – it's my treat. I forgot the lad's birthday, you see.'

She wasn't impressed. 'And you wouldn't want to disappoint your nephew a second time, would you?' she said, managing to make it sound as if she were just going along with a good wind-up.

'No, I mean it,' Paddy said earnestly. 'The lad's really looking forward to it. But I'll be back in time for the game . . . so how about it?'

'You'll just have to wait and see,' she said. 'I might have other plans by then.' She walked away, leaving Paddy a disappointed man.

He'd got over it by the next morning, when he met his brother, Danny and his son, Sam at the main gate.

They were sitting on the back of the car. 'Oy, faceache,' Danny called. Paddy grinned at them. Sam launched himself across the tarmac at him.

'Hold up, hold up,' Paddy said. 'Where's your salute?' He dropped his holdall.

Sam came to a version of attention not yet seen on any parade ground. He puffed out his chest and saluted. Paddy returned it. 'Good lad,' he said.

'You're a sergeant now, ain't you Paddy?' Sam asked.

'That's right, son,' Paddy said. 'Give us a hug.' He put his arms out, and Sam threw himself into them. Paddy swung him up – eleven or not, it didn't come amiss. 'Oh blimey – your cockney accent's coming along nicely, isn't it?' He put Sam down, and the lad grabbed his holdall and lugged it to the car.

Paddy followed him, but stopped to talk to his brother.

'I hope you've packed your sense of adventure,' Danny said. 'He's been going on about this nonstop ever since you came up with the idea.' He slammed the boot shut.

Paddy looked Danny over. Where Paddy was fair, his brother's hair was coppery, and he was heavily freckled. He was heavily set, too. 'You're getting a bit chubby, aren't you, Dan?' Paddy asked.

'Don't you start,' Danny said. 'I get enough of that from his mum.'

Paddy grabbed an inch of flab. 'Gives her something to hang on to,' he said.

Dan batted his hand away, they went round to the

front of the car; but before they could get in, Sergeant Hawkins came into the driveway. 'Sergeant Garvey!' she called.

'Sar'nt Hawkins,' Paddy said. He'd done a bit of discreet asking around, and had discovered that her first name was Sally.

She smiled and came over. 'So, this is your mythical brother and nephew,' she said.

'Believe me, now, do you?' Paddy said, doing a good job of hiding the fact that he was glad she'd turned up.

She pulled a sceptical face. 'Maybe,' she said. 'Hope you haven't forgotten a lunch box. Don't want you getting peckish.'

'Don't worry,' Dan put in. 'We'll look after him.'

'Make sure you do,' she said and smiled sweetly. 'The army can't operate without Sar'nt Garvey.' She looked up at him. 'Have a good time.' She walked away.

'Thanks. We will,' Paddy said, matching her tone for sarcasm.

Paddy and Dan turned to watch her go. 'Who's that?' Danny asked.

'Nobody – just a cook,' Paddy said, wondering why, if that were true, he felt so pleased to see her.

'Seems nice,' Dan said. He went and got in the driver's seat.

Yeah, Paddy thought. Pity she's got a tongue like a razor.


Spray sparkled in the air as Paddy rowed. The river

was cool and peaceful, overhung with trees and with only the rhythmic plash, plash, plash of the oars in the water to break the silence – that, and Sam's chatter.

'Paddy,' he grumbled. 'You said you could row.'

'Course I can,' Paddy said. 'I'm just used to the real thing, that's all – sat there in my rigid raider, with an elite team behind me with blackened faces, rowing silently towards some enemy-controlled beach-head – ' He remembered training in Cyprus. What Colour Sergeant Ryan would have made of that little tale he didn't know.

One thing was for sure – Danny wasn't impressed. 'You get a lot of enemy-controlled around Windsor, do you?' he asked lazily.

'Dad says all the army ever does is sit around and clean its boots,' Sam said.

'Oh does he?' Paddy said, knowing his brother was actually as proud of him as it was humanly possible to be.

'No I do not!' Dan protested. 'He's making it up – ' but he was grinning.

'Cheeky beggar!' Paddy dipped his hand into the water and splashed Danny, who grinned and got him back. When Paddy didn't respond, he did it again.

'Hey,' Danny said. Sam simply splashed some more.

Paddy dropped his oar and pointed at the lad. 'Easy,' he bellowed, in his best parade-ground voice and all three of them laughed.

A bit later, they came to a lock. Sam grabbed the

lock key and clambered out of the boat. They went through the first gate. To Paddy's surprise, Sam managed to open the sluice without too much trouble.

He started across the top of the lock gate. 'Easy, Sammy,' Paddy yelled. 'You fall in there and I'm not coming in after you – there's killer piranha in these waters.'

Sammy just grinned. He got across safely and ran to sort out the other gate.

'Go on, Sam,' Dan shouted. He turned to Paddy. 'Or we'll never get to that pub. You fancy a pint, don't you, Pad?'

'Yeah,' Paddy agreed. 'I could do with a breather, but don't tell him that.'

Dan watched the lad as he heaved open the down-river gate. He smiled affectionately. 'He thinks the world of you, you know.'

'I wish I'd spent more time with him when he was younger – ' It hadn't been possible – there'd been Northern Ireland and Hong Kong, and even postings in Britain hadn't taken him all that close to home.

'I wouldn't worry about it,' Dan said. 'It doesn't stop you being his favourite uncle.'

'Yeah?' Paddy asked. He'd known, of course – it was just startling to hear it said aloud.

'All those postcards you sent him?' Dan asked him over the rushing of the water. 'He's got them plastered all over his wall. Be more than my life's worth if I was so much as to touch 'em.'

Paddy couldn't help grinning. He thought to himself, I want one just like that. And a daughter too, of course . . .

171

Later, they pitched up near the pub, and because Sam wanted it, Paddy put up the little A-frame tent he'd brought along. He pulled the canopy up over the skiff, too – now that he wasn't rowing, it was hot in the sun. While Dan went off to the pub, he showed Sam how to do a reconnaissance, and they did a pretend Fibua exercise on the ruined church that stood nearby.

By the time Dan came back, Sam was curled up asleep in Paddy's arms – and Paddy wasn't so far off, himself.

'You've tired him out,' Dan said. He handed Paddy a can.

'He's a great kid, you know, Danny,' Paddy said.

Dan looked affectionately at his son. 'Yeah,' he agreed. 'When you think what we were like at that age . . .' he let his voice trail off, then popped his can and took a long swig.

'Wreaking havoc every weekend at the Saturday morning pictures,' Paddy agreed. 'I'd forgotten that – funny isn't it? Sometimes you only remember the bad stuff.' He ran his fingers through Sam's hair, suddenly sure it was as close as he'd ever get to looking after a son of his own.

Dan turned serious. 'Don't let the past put you off, Paddy – I know we weren't much of a family, but when it comes to starting your own it's a different kettle of fish, somehow – '

'No,' Paddy cut in. 'I had my chance with Nancy. That didn't work out.' He'd been sure he was over her. So why was his throat tightening up?

172

'Don't give me that, Paddy,' Danny said. 'You've got loads of time. You'll get another chance.' Paddy stared at him, sombrely. 'That is,' Danny added, 'if you want it enough.'

'Yeah, maybe you're right,' Paddy said, but he added mentally, I don't think so, though.

A bit later, they finished their beers and set off for home. Sam woke up and was as full of beans as if he'd slept a full eight hours. They made good time until they came to the lock again.

'Don't worry,' Dan said. 'We'll have you back in plenty of time for your footie.' Sam took the lock key again and climbed out to see to the gate, but this time Dan said, 'Hey Sammy — give your uncle the key.'

Paddy started to get out of the boat.

'Oh let me do it,' Sam said. He sounded fractious.

Paddy, wanting the day to end happily, sat back. 'Go on,' he said. He shrugged. 'It's the only way he'll learn,' he said to Dan.

Sam went to the gate. He put the key, which was basically a giant Allen key, into the hole. Whoever had been through last had done a good job of locking up behind them. Sam's face contorted as he struggled to make the key move.

'You want a hand with that?' Paddy called, lying back in the skiff.

'I can do it,' Sam shouted. He put all his weight on the key. It slipped out of the hole and out of his hands, and splashed into the water. Sam wobbled on the edge of the gate. Paddy was on his feet and ready to dive in after him, but the lad regained his balance.

He stared mournfully at the water. All that could be seen of the key was a few bubbles that floated on the scummy surface. 'Sorry,' he said.

'All right, Sergeant,' Danny said. 'You're the resourceful one – what do we do now?'

'Well, if we had a fishing rod, we could fish for it,' Paddy said. 'But we haven't, so why don't you go and find a nice long stick?'

Danny and Sam went off, leaving Paddy to guard the skiff. They were away a good long time, but they came back empty-handed. Paddy supposed he'd got so used to deliberately unkempt army training grounds that he'd forgotten a managed woodland would be quite different.

'What now?' Dan asked.

'Revert to Plan B,' Paddy said. Sam looked excited. 'We wait,' he explained.

And they did, for a good couple of hours, until a young couple came down the river. They thought it was a grand joke, especially when Sam blurted out that Paddy was an army sergeant.

'You mean you couldn't make a key out of spit and an old bootlace?' the bloke asked.

'No,' Paddy said sourly. 'That's the Royal Engineers.' By his calculations, the game would be well into injury time now, if they hadn't already got down the pub.

All in all, he wasn't terribly happy by the time Dan dropped him off outside the base, and the strain of trying to pretend for Sam's sake that he didn't mind only made it worse.

He crossed the road and went in the gate, trying to figure out exactly what he was going to say to Stubbs . . . and Brucie . . . and Voce.

But all of that went out of his mind as he was stopped at the gate. The guard had been tripled. 'What's going on, mate?' he asked the sergeant on duty.

'Security alert,' the man said. 'Some baby went AWOL half way through the five-a-side,' he said, as if it were of no importance.

It took a second to register. Then he thought: Lauren. My God. Tony. Joy. He ran. Someone, somewhere, had to be able to tell him what was going on. At the very least he could help the search.

He found Eddie and Sally – apparently, she'd taken his place in goal when he didn't show – outside the Naafi.

'Okay,' he said, breathing deep and hard. 'Where's Tony now?'

A few fusiliers trotted past, clearly in a search pattern. 'Married quarters,' Eddie said. 'They whizzed him and Joy away pretty smart.' There was clearly something working on him, but Paddy didn't have time to worry about that.

'I've got to see him,' Paddy said.

'You can't just charge over there,' Sally said. She turned to face him, and Paddy suddenly realized that she might not have known them long, but she was still concerned; he warmed to her.

That didn't mean she was right, though. 'Just leave it a while,' she said. Eddie nodded agreement.

There was no getting through to them. Paddy dumped his holdall on the ground, suddenly furious, not at them, but at the situation. If he couldn't see Tony and Joy, at least he could try and help. 'What sort of bastard person does a thing like this?' he demanded. If it had been Sammy – 'Come on, Eddie – you used to be a copper. Who'd want to steal someone else's baby?' Eddie just stared at him blankly. Again, Paddy got the feeling that something was working on him. 'I'm sorry,' Paddy said. 'This is useless. I've got to see him.' He picked his bag up and started back to the main gate.

'Wait!' Sally's voice came from behind him. He turned. 'I'll give you a lift.'

An odd expression passed across Eddie's face, and he walked off towards the company office. I'll catch up with him later, Paddy decided. For now he was just glad of Sally's company.

Paddy found Tony sitting beside Lauren's cot. It was in the nursery he'd half killed himself to finish before Joy got home from the hospital.

Paddy leaned on the door jamb. 'Hiya, mate,' he said. 'How you doing?'

Tony turned his head to look at him as if it were as heavy as lead. 'Uh . . . Joy's sleeping. The doctor's given her something.'

That was typical of him, Paddy thought: they might have their ups and downs, but as far as Tony was concerned, Joy came first and last, and in all positions between. 'How about *you*?' he insisted.

Tony got up and walked round to the end of the cot. He leaned on it, staring down as if he could somehow magic his daughter up out of nothing. 'People keep expecting me to go mad – to crack up or something,' he said. He stared at Paddy for a long moment. He was still in his football kit, and beneath his tan his skin had an odd greyish look to it. He turned back to the cot. 'I just feel weird. It's like everything's going in slow motion.' He leaned forward and put his weight on his forearms. 'I mean, I'm devastated. But I can't cry.' He laughed. 'My mouth – my mouth keeps going dry.'

He's in shock, Paddy thought. In shock and as near hysterics as we're ever going to see him. He moved into the room. 'Listen, mate – they're going to get Lauren back.' Tony stared at him. His eyes were flat and unreadable. 'She'll be okay.'

It was the wrong thing to say. Tony looked away. 'Paddy, I couldn't bear it.' His voice was thick with unshed tears. 'Taking her into church in a little white shoebox. I couldn't bear it.'

'Tony,' Paddy said fiercely, 'that's not going to happen.' I'll make it not happen, he thought. I'll find a way.

'She was so precious,' Tony said. He laughed again, a short, unpleasant bark. 'You know what the police said to me?' He looked at Paddy with outraged eyes. 'They said, "Can you afford to have her?" I mean you don't think about that, do you?' Paddy didn't answer. He didn't have any words adequate to respond to such anguish. 'You just think about them as your family – about how they're always going to be around.'

'I know,' Paddy said. 'I know – I understand.' But he knew he didn't, not really. He didn't think you could, unless you'd been through it, known what it was like to hold a child of your body in your arms: and he thought that maybe he never would have a chance to find out.

A door slammed somewhere in the house.

'Joy!' Tony called. He pushed past Paddy, who could only follow him through to the kitchen.

Joy was in there. She looked dreadful – wan and red-eyed. She'd got her food mixer out, and was going through the cupboard, getting packets out.

'What you doing, love?' Tony asked.

'It's Miss Butler's wedding cake,' Joy replied. 'I said I'd do the icing for it.'

Tony went towards her. 'You don't have to do it now, darlin',' he said. But it was just typical of Joy, as Paddy had seen over and over again – the more upset she was, the harder she worked.

'Can't keep leaving it, can I?' Joy said. She cracked an egg expertly, with one hand, into a bowl. 'Don't want to let her down.' A second egg followed the first, but this time she dropped the shell in. She fished it out.

Tony took another step towards her and put his hands out as if to cuddle her; but at the last minute, he let them hover above her shoulders, as if she would shatter if he touched her. Or explode, more like, Paddy thought.

'Stop,' Tony said. 'Stop now, darling –' he looked at Paddy and jerked his head in a clear gesture for him to leave.

Paddy went. He heard Tony murmur something; and then Joy. There was a wet slapping sound as something hit the wall. That, he thought, is probably a good sign. He glanced in at the kitchen window as he walked by. Tony and Joy were holding on to each other as if they would disintegrate if they didn't.

Which, Paddy thought sadly, was more or less true.

Sally was waiting for him by the car. He went and leaned on its roof, chin on arms.

'Are they all right?' Sally asked.

'I don't know,' Paddy said. 'How do you deal with it? How do you prepare for it?'

Sally touched him gently on the shoulder. 'You can't,' she said. 'Nobody can.' She rubbed his arm. 'Come on, soldier-boy. I'll take you back to base and we'll see if there's anything else we can do to help.'

But there wasn't. Paddy found Eddie drinking in the Naafi. He had his tail between his legs. He explained quietly that he'd thought Melanie might have taken Lauren – he'd tried to break things off with her before the game, and she'd been upset. He'd told the RMPs, and they'd found her by the river. She hadn't even known the little girl was missing – and she'd been outraged when she realized Eddie was accusing her.

'So it's all over between you then?' Paddy asked. 'That was what you wanted, wasn't it?' He sipped

179

his pint. Normally he wouldn't have been in the Naafi at all – sergeants were expected to stick to their own mess. But he still didn't know many people there, and he didn't feel like drinking alone.

'Yeah,' Eddie said. 'I just didn't want to hurt her so badly to do it.'

'Take it from me, mate, sometimes there is no other way.' Paddy shifted back on the red leatherette of his seat.

They got another round in. It was amazing how slowly time could pass, Paddy decided. It felt like they'd been there whole days, but in fact it was more like an hour or so. The trouble was, neither of them could think of a thing to say.

Suddenly, Sally appeared at his side. 'Paddy! I've been looking all over for you!'

'What?' he said. 'Lauren?' He felt his heart pound against his ribs.

'She's safe,' Sally said. 'Your CSM's daughter took her –'

'Sarah?' Eddie said. He looked a bit bewildered.

'She got herself in the club a while back,' Paddy explained. 'She's only a kid –'

'Made her get rid of it, did they?' Sally asked. Her eyes glinted.

'I don't know the rights of it,' Paddy said impatiently. 'For all I know it was her idea. Now tell me about Lauren.'

'She's back with Joy and Tony –' Sally said. 'Well – what are you waiting for? Don't you want a lift?'

Paddy stood up. 'You coming, Eddie?' he asked.

'Later,' Eddie said. 'I don't know them so well, and I've got some thinking to do.'

'All right,' Paddy said. He looked at Eddie's half-empty glass. 'Just make sure it's thinking, not drinking.'

Lauren was more beautiful than Paddy remembered her. Tony was right – she was precious. As for Joy, she looked absolutely radiant.

'Got another job, I have,' Tony said, after he'd told Paddy the whole story of how Stubbsie had found Sarah nursing Lauren in her bedroom

'Oh yeah?' Paddy asked. He finished his cup of tea.

'Redecorating the kitchen to get the egg stains off the walls,' he answered.

'Tony!' Joy said.

Paddy stood up. Tony picked Matthew up and followed him out. They stood blinking in the bright sunshine.

'You sure you won't stay for a beer?' Tony asked.

'I would, mate, but I'm on a pizza and a promise.' He pointed across the carpark, where Sally was leaning against her motor. She waved at him.

'Oh right!' Tony said, clearly surprised. Paddy started to walk away. 'Well, listen,' Tony added. 'Thanks for coming round.'

Paddy slapped him lightly on the arm. They both knew he meant earlier, not now. 'Don't mention it,' he said, and again turned to walk away.

He only got a couple of yards before Tony called

out to him. 'Paddy, Joy was talking earlier on –'
Paddy turned. He crossed his arms and waited,
knowing that if it was taking Tony ages to get to the
point it was probably worth hearing. 'She was thinking about getting Lauren christened, and well –' he
stopped. Definitely worth hearing, Paddy thought.
'She wondered if you wanted to be the godfather.'

'Me?' Paddy asked. He was delighted. 'I'd really
love to, mate.' He felt a smile that would have done
the Cheshire cat proud spread across his face.
'That'd be great.'

Tony grinned back at him. 'I said it was a crap
idea. But you know – what she wants, she gets.'

Paddy could only nod. His throat had closed up,
and he realized he was close to tears. Just then, Joy
came out carrying Lauren.

'Come on, Matthew,' she said. 'Bath time.' The
lad turned and held out his arms to her.

Tony shoved his hand out, and Paddy shook it.
'Take care, Sarge,' he said. It was the first time he'd
called Paddy that.

'Thanks, Tony,' he said. They both smiled at him.
'Joy,' he said, feeling suddenly awkward. 'That's
really nice that is.'

He backed away a couple of paces – they seemed
so happy he hated to stop looking at them – then
turned and walked across to the car where Sally was
waiting for him.

'I'm going to be a godfather,' he announced, just a
touch smugly, as he slid into the passenger seat
beside her.

Sally looked up at him. She raised her eyebrows. 'Oh yeah?' she asked. He nodded happily. 'You know you're trouble, don't you?' she asked, and answered before he could say anything. 'You're broody, Paddy Garvey.'

# Chapter 8

It was possibly the hardest assignment Paddy had ever been given in all his time in the army.

He stared down at the plump little man who had spoken to him. 'You have to help me,' the man said again. He ran his hand through his thinning silvery hair. 'You have to make sure my son's okay —'

Paddy sighed. 'All right, Tommy,' he said at last, although he knew he was going to regret it. 'We'll get Major Voce through his stag night in one piece.'

'Thank you,' Mr Voce said. 'All I want is to get my son to the altar tomorrow upright and *compos mentis* — and if that best man of his has his way, he won't be either.'

'We'll see to it,' Paddy said. He strode over to the pool table, where Dave and Joe had just started a game. 'All right, lads. Pin back your ears — we have a special assignment.'

I'm going to regret this, he thought. Sally'll kill me and I'll never be able to look Major Voce in the eye again.

He took a pull on his pint. Oh well, he told himself. I never did want to make CSM anyway.

They piled into Joe's minicab. Paddy might not have

approved of it, but Joe had long since stopped arguing with Dave, and his cabbing didn't seem to affect his work, so Paddy had stopped worrying about it.

As they were about to drive off, Mr Voce appeared. He thrust a rolled up wad of notes through the open window at Paddy.

'Tommy, we don't want your money,' Paddy said. 'Go home and get some beauty sleep.'

'Take it,' Mr Voce insisted. He sighed. 'Call it expenses. Or buy some flowers for that girl you stood up.'

Dave leaned forward from his seat in the back. He grabbed the money. 'Go on then, you've twisted my arm,' he said.

Paddy rounded on him. 'I don't believe you, Dave.'

'Yes, well, I've already made a prat of myself once today, so I might as well make it twice,' Dave said.

Joe pulled out and contacted his minicab office.

'What?' Paddy asked Dave.

'Went to see that art teacher of Donna's.' He scowled. 'Asked him what was going on.'

'Aren't you being just a bit paranoid, Dave?' Paddy asked. But he knew that Dave had been fretting for weeks about it, ever since Donna had started going to the classes. Maybe it was better for him to get it out of his system.

'Oh, he takes my wife to art galleries, buys her and my kid ice creams – nothing to worry about there – ' Dave said, with sarcasm so heavy it could have crushed a ten-ton truck. 'Anyway, he said nothing had happened. So I've nothing to worry about. And I'm a happy man.'

He looked far from happy, but there was no time to talk about it any more, because Joe's radio crackled into life. 'Someone's ordered a number of cabs in the name of Voce,' said a female voice through heavy static. 'Heading in convoy to the Veranda wine bar.'

'Bullseye,' Joe said.

Dave tucked the money into his top pocket. It seemed to cheer him up. 'Anyway, Eddie and Tony are missing out,' he said.

'Yeah right,' Paddy said, realizing with a sinking heart that he was probably going to be bringing two drunks home that night. 'Who needs a fortnight's leave when you could be stuck in here with us.'

'Why don't we just look for a trail of upper-class vomit?' Dave asked. 'Only sick for miles with maraschino cherries in it.'

'Very good, Dave,' Paddy said. It set the tone of the evening nicely.

'Elementary, my dear Watson,' Dave said, in an accent that indicated he was getting ready to hobnob.

It took them a little while to get there. It was a very nice place – all potted fig trees and pretty signs outside. It was far too small for them to go into without Voce spotting them.

'Here we are, lads,' Paddy said. He and Joe looked through the window. 'Target located.'

The major and his cronies were clustered around the bar. They were still on pints instead of shorts, which was something.

'Hanging baskets,' Dave said in a disgusted tone from behind him. He came to have a look inside too.

186

'Bar staff in uniforms,' Paddy muttered.

'He'll be safe enough here,' Joe said.

'I reckon so,' Paddy agreed. But then he saw one of the crowd – not someone he knew, but at a guess the best man – unscrew a hip-flask and pour a generous dose of spirits into a pint, then hand it to Voce. 'Uh oh,' he said. 'Little Mickey Finn just made an appearance.'

They retreated to the car to keep watch. Sure enough, after an hour or so Voce came out. He was almost walking straight, and his tie was only adrift of smart by an inch or so, so it was really only the flush in the cheeks that gave him away.

They tailed the party at a discreet distance – so discreet that the major's party had already gone in by the time they got there. It was a moderately hole-in-the-wall joint. A neon sign outside proclaimed it to be the *Cage D'Or*.

'Cage de rust, more like,' Dave said as they went in. The entrance fees cost them a chunk of the money Tommy had given them, and Dave immediately used some more of it to buy a round. The major seemed to be doing okay, Paddy thought. He didn't want to spoil all the man's fun – a stag night was a stag night, after all. He sipped at his drink and admired the scenery – which, if you liked acres of female flesh, was pretty good.

He suddenly realized that Dave had disappeared. He decided not to let that distract him – then it struck him that he couldn't see the major, either. He pushed his way through the crowd to get a better view of the dance floor. Nothing, but then it was packed. He moved around again, and saw Dave approaching from the bar, bopping in time to the music as he came. He was carrying the largest cocktail Paddy had ever seen. The decorations included three umbrellas, four cherries on sticks, a little fake flower and a sparkler. He sucked at the drink through a straw.

'How many of those have you had?' Paddy asked.

'Who's counting?' Dave replied. 'I'm preserving cover.' He watched two girls walk by. Preserving cover did not seem to be on their agenda – not given the handkerchiefs they were wearing as dresses. 'Camouflage,' Dave explained.

A movement out on the dance floor caught Paddy's eye. 'I do not like the look of that,' he said.

Major Voce was dancing with a blonde girl whose main aim in life seemed to be to remove his shirt. Paddy had seen surgical gloves that were looser than her top. At least it's a fast dance, he thought. But even as he watched, she threw her arms round his neck and nuzzled up close.

'Take paint remover to get her off him, it will,' Joe said.

'We'd better do something,' Paddy said.

'Uh, chaps?' Dave said. Paddy felt a tug on his arm. He turned round in time to see Dave bending over clutching his stomach.

He sighed. 'Come on, Joe – we'd better get him to the bog.' He glanced at the major, who was still firmly attached to the blonde girl.

They dragged Dave off between them. They stood

outside the stalls, listening to the impressive range of groans and grunts that came from inside.

'Name that tune,' Paddy said.

'Come on, Dave,' Joe called.

Eventually, Dave came out. He was covered in sweat but at least his dark shirt still looked fairly clean. 'I can't remember eating half that,' he said cheerfully. 'Anyway, I'm fine now,' he added. He sprayed his mouth with breath freshener. 'Carry on drinking?' he asked hopefully.

'I used to look up to him, you know,' Paddy said to Joe, who looked at him disbelievingly. Smart man, Joe Farrell.

They went back out to the dance floor, but the major's party had gone. At least the blonde girl had found another partner. Dave headed for the bar.

'Oh no you don't,' Paddy said. He grabbed Dave by the scruff of the neck and propelled him towards the exit. A girl in a red silk blouse looked at them quizzically. 'Underage, don't you know, ma'am,' Paddy said.

Outside, a gale was blowing up. 'This'll make them easier to find,' Joe said confidently. Paddy gave him a blank look. 'Rotten night – keep the punters in. Our beloved major and his mates'll be the only idiots out there. You'll see.'

But they didn't. They drove around for a good three quarters of an hour before Joe's control finally said, 'Large party name of Voce dropped off at the Banana Club, Salter Street.'

The *Banana Club*, Paddy thought. He could just imagine.

It was even worse than that. This time, several of the neon letters didn't work, and a pink sign underneath said, *strippers*.

'Whahay the lads,' Dave said rubbing his hands together.

'You can leave the stage Geordie out, Dave,' Paddy said. 'The real one's bad enough.'

They went in. A wall of sound hit them — music so loud it was distorted, and a cacophony of jeers and cheers and whistles. Paddy extracted the last of Tommy's money from Dave's top pocket and paid their entrance fees.

They found themselves on a gallery, overlooking a stage, with rows of seats all around it. The seats were all filled, mostly with upper-class types with short hair. There was a woman on the stage. She was dressed — if you could call it that — in a black g-string and a feathered bustier, and very little else. Major Voce was also on the stage. He was stripped to the waist and covered in baby oil, and he was wearing a wedding veil. He had his face buried in the stripper's bustier, and she was eating a banana in a way that made it pretty clear what else she could be eating.

Nancy would've said this exploits women, Paddy thought; and heaven only knew what Sally would have said. But it looked to him pretty much as if the woman was in control down there.

'Oh my God,' he said.

'Gentlemen,' Joe said. 'I think it's time.'

They turned as one. They'd worked out what to do in the car, while they were trying to find the party.

'Look on the bright side,' Tucker said. 'At least he's still got his trousers on.'

They went downstairs and grabbed what they needed from the lobby. The ticket girl tried to stop them, but they moved too fast for her, and fortunately all the bouncers were inside watching Major Voce make a pranny of himself.

They went inside the main room. Major Voce was just about to have a very close encounter with the woman's bustier – or its contents.

'He who dares, wins,' Dave said loudly. A few men looked round. Dave held up the nozzle of the fire extinguisher he had liberated and turned it on. Foam poured out.

Paddy let Dave and Joe clear a path. Punters dived for cover left and right. Paddy charged through and leapt up on the stage.

The stripper glared at him. He put his hands round her waist and lifted her bodily off the stage. 'No disrespect, ma'am,' he said as she struggled. 'Any other time and I'd really enjoy this.'

He turned back to Major Voce, who had barely moved. 'I've come to take you away from all this, Sir,' he said. The major leaned forwards and tried to kiss him on the lips. 'No, you can't do that, Sir,' Paddy said as he hoisted him in a fireman's lift across his shoulders. 'It's Sergeant Garvey, Sir.'

He walked out, through the shambles that had once been the *Banana Club*. Dave and Joe provided rear cover for the tactical retreat – it was amazing, Paddy thought, how much foam you could get in one fire extinguisher.

Paddy knocked on Tommy Voce's door. Major Voce was slung between him and Dave. They'd got a shirt on him, but it wasn't buttoned, and he was still wearing the wedding veil. The door handle rattled. At the last moment, Dave whipped the veil off him and held it behind his back.

'God help Britain with you lot to defend her,' Mr Voce said.

Paddy realized that Major Voce's head was slumped over. He pushed it up.

'Hi dad,' said Major Voce. Then he fell over.

The next morning Lieutenant Forsythe had another special assignment for them. Last night's gale had blown an oak tree right across the drive of the hotel where the reception was to be held, and the electricity had also been cut off. The only hope for the wedding was if Four Platoon could get the mess sorted out in time.

Paddy oversaw the platoon loading a couple of trucks worth of equipment.

'Move,' he yelled as the men carried out a block and tackle. 'It's like watching paint dry!' Dave came out carrying a chainsaw in each hand. 'Don't strain yourself, Dave,' Paddy said. He still hadn't quite forgiven him for screwing up the night before.

Forsythe came out, dressed in his best blues and trying hard not to trip over his sword. 'I've rooted out a bloody good spark, and he's on his way to see if he can restore power to the hotel,' Brucie said.

'Well done, Sir,' Paddy said. 'The chainsaws are on board and Four Platoon are all yours.'

Brucie put his cap on and adjusted the highly polished peak. 'Right,' he said.

Farrell dashed up and saluted.

'Where the hell have you been, Farrell?' Paddy asked.

'What's up, Sarge?' Farrell asked instead of responding to the question.

'We have a chance to redeem ourselves,' Paddy said. 'Now get on the truck.'

They moved out.

The tree was lodged right across the entrance to the hotel. It had a huge crown, and it was immediately obvious that there would be no moving the trunk until the branches were stripped off. It was a long, hard, sweaty slog – but basically straightforward, although a bucket chain of chefs taking food in didn't help matters, and neither did having to find somewhere safe and shady to put several dozen table centrepieces of lilies and gypsophila.

By the time they were halfway done, Brucie's dress uniform was in a state of near total undress, his sword had twice been buried under a pile of discarded foliage, and for a while it looked as if he'd have to fork out for a new cap.

For all that, by the time the afternoon rolled around they were able to get lines on the main mass of the trunk. The lorry roared a protest as the driver gunned the engine.

'Tucker, Farrell,' Paddy yelled. 'Push the bloody thing.' They got in behind the trunk and pushed.

Knox and Lowery added their weight, and suddenly it was moving. There was an awful tearing sound as the trunk scraped across the tarmac, but the truck moved on.

A car engine purred in the distance.

'Give it some,' Paddy yelled. The truck engine revved. The men pushed.

'Much more of this and I'll be invalided out with a hernia,' Dave said. But he gave it another go.

The open-topped wedding car came into view. The truck pulled the trunk clear just in time for the car to sweep round into the driveway. It slowed to a halt, and Major Voce and the new Mrs Voce surveyed the chaos.

'What's going on here?' the major asked. If he were hung over, he was doing a good job of not showing it.

'Oh, it's nothing,' Brucie said. 'Just a little problem – Sooty could have sorted it out.'

Paddy frowned. Some in-joke, he supposed. He whispered to Dave, 'One good thing – he was so pissed he probably can't remember a thing about it.'

The major was so grateful to Four Platoon that he invited them all to the reception. Paddy wandered through the gardens with Joe and his girlfriend Colette, and Dave. Donna hadn't come.

'I asked her, Paddy,' Dave said. 'But she said no. When have you ever known my Donna turn down a night out? Said she couldn't get a sitter, but she always used to manage fine – '

'Well, Joy and Tony are on leave,' Paddy said. 'Maybe she couldn't think of anyone else.'

194

'It's not that,' Dave said gloomily. 'It's that art teacher fella. And she hasn't helped.' He gestured at Colette. She might be Joe's girlfriend, but she was also the manager of a local travel agent, and Donna had been fascinated by her ever since they were introduced.

'Oh give over, Dave,' Paddy said. 'You're jumping at shadows –'

'No, I'm not, Paddy,' Dave cut in. 'It's him. That art teacher. Mark bloody Owen.'

' – and you'll drive her away for sure if you keep this up,' Paddy finished.

'It's not me, it's her,' Dave insisted. 'I'm losing her, Paddy, and I don't know what to do about it.'

Colette came up to them. 'Oh cheer up, you two,' she said. 'Here, have a sausage on a stick – that'll shut you up.' She handed one to Dave. 'Could be worse, anyway,' she added. 'Look at him.' She pointed to a garden seat, where Brucie was sitting with his head in his hands.

They went over. 'Sir?' Paddy said. 'You all right, Sir?'

Forsythe looked up at him. 'I've got nothing left to give, Sergeant,' he said. He flopped back in the seat, letting the impact knock a sigh out of him.

Paddy stared at him, bemused.

Someone poked him on the arm. He turned. Major Voce's father stood there. 'Sergeant Garvey, you are just the fella,' he said.

'What's the problem?' Paddy asked.

But when he heard the answer, he rather wished he hadn't.

A few minutes later, he stood behind the stage in the main hall, staring at a pile of musical instruments. They'd arrived on an early plane, but the gales had grounded the band's flight out of Southern Ireland. Tommy's bright idea was for him – with a few volunteers – to take their place.

'Look,' he said. 'There's a pile of sheet music – all we've got to do is follow the melody.'

Paddy strummed the lead guitar. He fiddled with the keys. At least the thing was tuning up fairly easily. 'If you ask me I think we're being a bit over-ambitious,' he said.

Dave divided his attention between looking at some of the music and handling bits of drumkit to Colette, who was helping Voce's best man to set up.

'Don't be daft,' Tommy said. 'I'm king of the keyboards down the Legion, me – so as long as the best man can make shift on the drums, we'll be fine.'

Paddy wasn't convinced, but he could see he was beaten.

'Oh, my Joe's gorgeous on guitar,' Colette said. She smiled a particularly sloppy smile at him. She's up to something, Paddy thought.

Paddy leaned over to look at the music Dave was reading. 'It's like a bloody Cliff Richard film,' he said.

'Oh yeah,' Dave asked. 'Who's playing Cliff then?' He was just a bit smug about it.

'You are,' Paddy said, 'and you know it.' He shoved another sheet into Dave's hand. 'I'll do the harmonies,' he said.

'Chin up,' Dave said. 'We know some of these – remember that music-hall show they roped us into a couple of years back?'

Paddy did. It hadn't been a total disaster. Singing was one of Dave's talents he simply didn't get to show off very often.

They had a few minutes to go over things, though – but they were startled out of it by the sight of Colette proposing to Joe. She'd even bought him a ring to give to her.

Paddy frowned. 'How many times has she turned him down?'

'Four, I think,' Dave said. 'Here, you don't think he'll say yes, do you?'

'Don't ask stupid questions, Dave,' Paddy said as Colette and Joe went into the tightest clinch since Major Voce met the stripper.

Forsythe went on stage to announce them.

'Come on, lover boy,' Paddy said to Joe. 'We're on.'

They got in position just as Brucie said, 'Ladies and gentlemen – I give you tonight's very special guests: the Band of Gold.'

The curtains swept open. Paddy got the mike in position. It hummed alarmingly. There'd been no time at all for anything as sophisticated as a sound check. He looked round at the audience. There was a scattering of applause, but Major Voce and the ex-Miss Butler were wearing expressions of extreme consternation, not to say panic.

'Thank you very much,' he said.

'Good evening, London,' Dave cut in. 'It's good to be back.'

'Ladies and gentlemen,' Paddy went on. The Major and Mrs Voce were whispering together. 'Bride and Groom,' he added. That got their attention. 'I give you – The Unrighteous Brothers.' It was a bad joke, and Brucie had already introduced them as the Band of Gold, but it did wonders for Paddy's nerves.

They launched into the first song – 'Unchained Melody'. The intro played, and Dave started to come in too early. Paddy shook his head and he stopped in time. Then he came in right on the money. There was a renewed scattering of applause, and Paddy saw Mrs Voce start to smile. The major led her down to the dance floor. Paddy came in with his harmonies, and suddenly he was enjoying himself.

So was Dave, he thought – singing like an angel, singing for Donna who wasn't even there to hear him. Hear him, Donna, Paddy thought. Wherever you are, hear him. Don't leave him. He'll never cope without you.

# Chapter 9

Paddy stood in the forecourt of Buckingham Palace. He had just received his Queen's Gallantry medal, and his head was still spinning from it. Sooner or later he knew he'd think it through and work out what had happened when and who had said what to whom, but for now it was all he could do to pose for the pictures his brother Danny wanted to take. He put his arm round his nephew Sam's shoulders, and smiled as the camera churred and clicked.

Then the smile turned even broader as he saw Sally walking across the gravel towards him. She was wearing an ankle-length floral sundress that some-how made her boyish figure look very girlish.

'Congratulations, Sergeant,' she said. Her smile lit up her face and put dimples in her cheeks.

'Thank you, Sergeant,' he replied, and added, 'you look gorgeous.'

'Ooh!' Sally said. 'You don't look so bad yourself.'

Paddy grinned. He hoped he was doing his dress uniform proud. 'You know my brother Danny,' he said, gesturing at the copper-haired man wielding the camera. 'His little boy, Sam.' Sally came over and shook his hand. The lad was all done up too – in his school uniform.

'Queen's Gallantry medal, huh?' Sally said. He held it out from the other medals he was wearing on his chest. 'I feel quite proud of you, Paddy.' She turned slightly, and Dan took another picture. 'So, what did the Queen say?'

'Oh, you know, very informal – "Hiya Paddy. How's it going? Don't tread on the corgi."' That made her smile, which pleased him.

'Twit,' she said. She went up on tiptoes to kiss him, and that set Dan off again with the camera.

Tony, Eddie and Dave walked past in their ceremonial uniforms. 'Congratulations, Paddy,' Tony called.

'Well done, mate,' Eddie added.

'Shut up – you know I didn't do anything,' Paddy said.

'No we didn't mean the piece of tin,' Tony called from behind Dan. He pointed with a white-gloved hand. 'We meant Sally.'

Her mouth tightened – just slightly, but it was there all the same. It didn't help that the three of them burst into a quick chorus of *Mr and Mrs*.

'I'm sorry about that,' Paddy said. At least she was smiling. 'Bastards,' he added under his breath.

That little incident set Paddy thinking, though. He realized that he hardly knew Sally, though they'd been together several months – and that he was hardly likely to get to know her while he was living in the mess. Besides, he was tired of living cheek by jowl with people he worked with every day.

He applied for, and got, permission to live out. It

took time to find what he was looking for – something he could afford, and that was within easy travelling of the base, and yet that he could put his mark on. He wanted to make the place really his own.

The fifth place he saw turned out to be ideal. It was a self-contained attic flat in an old half-timbered house. The whole place was being renovated, but they were doing it slowly and hadn't got to the attic so far.

As soon as he walked in, he knew he had to have it. The rooms were large and airy, with big windows and ceilings high enough that even the sloped parts didn't make him feel hemmed in.

'I'll take it,' he said.

There was trouble on the base that night – CSM Stubbs' son was in training at the depot, but he absconded and turned up at Dave and Donna's. Paddy was too busy packing to take much notice, and besides, he presumed it would all work itself out in the end. Besides, he'd decided to give Dave a wide berth for the time being – he'd be there if his friend needed him, but he didn't want to be accused of sticking his nose in where it wasn't wanted. In any case, he was worried that any advice he gave might be the wrong thing – he didn't exactly have the world's greatest record in the marriage stakes.

The next day, he took Sally round to the flat, but all he told her was that he had a surprise for her. She looked dubious as they got out of the car, and even more dubious as she walked up the stairs.

He pushed open the door and let her go in past him.

'What's this, Paddy?' she asked, looking round with interest.

'It's a flat.'

'I know,' she said. 'I meant, whose flat is it?' She walked into the front room, past the cans of paint he'd bought that morning.

Gawd, he thought. Between the lads the other day, and now this, she probably thinks I'm going to propose. Not that the thought hadn't crossed his mind, but he knew it was way too early for that. 'It's my flat,' he said in a tone that, he hoped, left no room for doubt. 'I told you I was getting fed up with the mess, so I thought, "Sod it – why not move out, get my own place."'

'You don't waste any time, do you?' she said, and smiled. She walked over to the big dormer window that was one of the room's best features.

'I know it needs a lick of paint, but I'm dead chuffed with it,' he said. Even if I can lean on some parts of the ceiling, he thought, as he realized his hand was resting on one of the inward slopes of the roof.

'Yeah,' Sally said. She didn't sound totally convinced.

Now for the tricky bit, Paddy thought. 'I just want you to know that you're welcome to come round here whenever you like,' he said. Don't let her think I'm propositioning her, he thought silently.

'Right,' she said warily. 'Thank you.' The sun

struck copper from the chestnut highlights in her hair.

Paddy walked over to her. 'Don't worry,' he said, hoping he sounded reassuring. 'I'm not asking you to move in.' He took a deep breath. 'I just want to know you better, Sal. And if you'd like that too, then we need a bit of space to do it properly.' He looked at her anxiously. Her expression was unreadable, as it so often was. 'What you thinking?' he asked.

'I'll tell you what I'm thinking,' she said. 'If you're so keen to get to know me better, there are one or two things you've forgotten – '

'Like what?' he asked. He couldn't think of anything she'd ever said was important to her.

'Like a table, chairs, curtains, carpets – ' she looked at him slyly, and began to grin. She obviously realized her wind-up had worked. 'A cooker so you can make me delicious meals – '

'And a bed,' Paddy said. It had to be worth a go, and in truth the fact that they hadn't slept together was beginning to get to him. But seeing the expression on her face, he added quickly, 'Just in case you've had a few too many one night and want to get your head down here.'

Sally patted him on the arm. 'One step at a time,' she said.

'Absolutely,' Paddy said, thinking, damn damn damn.

He spent his off-duty hours over the next couple of days painting, choosing warm, rich colours – deep sea-green for the living room, and a rich yellow for the bedroom.

While he painted, Paddy had plenty of time to think about Dave's situation with Donna. It seemed to be going from bad to worse. She'd even gone off for a week on some art course in Brighton. He'd had a go at talking to Dave about it, but the man did a good impersonation of a clamshell.

As for Jack Stubbs, he'd spent a couple of days hanging round the base, and more particularly with Eddie and Dave. That sounded like getting into bad habits to Paddy, but he didn't feel it was his place to intervene. It wasn't as if the CSM didn't know Dave's reputation. Besides, the lad had made the right decision and gone back to the depot in the end, so it had all worked out.

The painting didn't take long, but then, he didn't bother with undercoat, much less primer. When he was done, he went out on a shopping spree. After all, he had to strike while the iron was hot.

After that, there was nothing left for it but to invite Sally round for dinner. He hadn't realized how nervous he was about it until she knocked on the door and his mouth went dry as she walked in.

She looked round open-mouthed. 'Well,' she said. 'You've been busy.'

'Just a bit,' he said. He'd managed to find a single armchair, some rugs and curtains and a decent coffee table large enough to eat off. A few pictures from the market, a vase with some dried grass in it, and suddenly the place looked like home.

Sally took a bottle of white wine from her bag.

'You needn't have done that,' Paddy said as he took it from her.

'Already chilled, seeing as you don't have a fridge,' she said, 'and I didn't really fancy warm Liebfraumilch.'

Paddy grinned. Then a horrible thought crossed his mind. 'Oh shit,' he said.

'What's the matter?' Sally asked.

'I haven't got a corkscrew.'

'Oh no,' Sally exclaimed. She was obviously upset that they weren't going to be able to drink her present. You berk, Garvey, Paddy thought at himself.

Then Sally produced a corkscrew from her bag.

'You are a real trooper,' Paddy said. 'I'll get some glasses.' He started to walk away, but Sally pulled him back.

'Uh uh,' she said. 'I want a kiss first.'

'You want too much too soon,' Paddy protested.

'That's an order, *Acting* Sergeant Garvey.'

'You're ruthless,' he said.

'I know.'

'All right,' he said. 'An order's an order.' He kissed her gently on the mouth, then broke away. 'Things you do for your country, hey?' He kissed her again.

Eventually, he decided he'd better go and dish dinner up before it spoiled.

Afterwards, they sat in the glow of the candles he'd lit.

'That was so good,' Sally said. 'I'm impressed.'

Paddy poured them both another glass of wine. 'Yeah, it wasn't bad, was it?' he said. 'Even if I say so myself.'

'You'll be after my job soon,' Sally said, and sipped her wine.

'No, I don't think so.' Paddy stared at her seriously. 'I'm only good for one dish.'

That made her laugh. 'Oh – I nearly forgot!' She reached into her bag and took out a flat parcel wrapped in red foil. 'I've brought you a flat-warming present.'

'You're like Father Christmas, you are,' Paddy said. He took the gift and tore the paper off. He pulled out something made of blue cloth, and it took him a second to realize it was a sheet; and a second more to work out the implication. 'Sheets!' he said.

He was still trying to decide if she meant what he thought she did when she said, 'Yeah, sheets. I bet you're using some manky old sleeping bag.' She got up and headed towards the bedroom.

He followed her, and got there just in time to see the look of surprise on her face when she saw the bed with its luxury linen and the fan he'd fastened to the wall above it. He'd turned the quilt down, more in hope than expectation.

'Wonders will never cease,' she said.

He leaned on the wall behind her, so close he could smell her perfume. 'You see I'm quite cultured, really,' he said.

She eyed the turned-back quilt. 'Are you expecting somebody?' she asked.

'No,' he lied, thinking, damn. You blew it, Garvey. You bloody blew it. To cover his embarrassment, he said, 'So, you want a coffee?'

'You're not supposed to say that,' she said.

'Pudding?' he asked, wondering how she always managed to keep him so off-balance. She swung round to face him, but didn't answer. 'What am I supposed to say?' he asked.

She put her finger on his lips. 'Nothing,' she said.

He put his hand on her hand and kissed her very lightly on the lips. 'It's just as well,' he said, walking towards her so she had to move back.

'Why?' she asked, giggling.

'I don't have any coffee,' he said, and they fell together on the bed; and after that neither of them said anything for a long, long time.

# Chapter 10

A couple of days after Paddy had got the flat to his liking, he was asked to select a couple of men to accompany him on a week's adventure training. He picked Knox, and after a couple of minutes thought, Dave. He still hadn't worked out what the matter was, but he reckoned that some time away from Donna would do Dave the world of good.

He was wrong – Dave fretted constantly. He misread maps while orienteering, dropped his paddle during the whitewater canoeing and almost caused a real disaster with a bad bit of rope management when he went abseiling.

All in all, it took the edge off the week for Paddy – everything Dave did came back on him – and he was glad to get home. Almost as soon as he arrived, he was assigned to Junior NCO cadre duty. Tony was also assigned to it, and Joe and Dave were up for it. And again, Dave did somewhere between terribly and appallingly. Paddy could only hope he'd redeem himself in the final Fibua exercise – a full-scale attack on a defended building. It was one often used by the army for such exercises.

Colonel Jennings was to be present throughout, and he briefed the senior NCOs and his junior officers from the steps of the old mansion they would be using. 'This is the main task for tomorrow. From the ambush stand each section will move on to this building, where they will encounter strong enemy resistance.' He glanced around at the mansion. 'Now, as you can see from the size of the building, there's a lot for the attacking forces to get their teeth into — lots of rooms to clear, lots of places they can be surprised in. And I'm sure Mr Forsythe and Sar'nt Garvey will make this a worthwhile test of our budding NCOs. Right Jeremy?'

'Sir,' Forsythe said quietly.

'Good! No point in letting them just stroll in and help themselves,' Jennings finished. 'Right, gentlemen. Follow me.' He led the way inside.

The others had a brief look round then left, but Paddy and Lieutenant Forsythe had to go over the place in detail. He was checking the exits from one of the front rooms when the lieutenant called him out into the corridor.

'Yes, Sir?' he said as he came out.

'Could a counter attack withdraw through those rooms, or are they all dead ends?' Brucie asked. He pointed down the corridor, to a section where doors led off to left and right.

They went into the area he was talking about, walking past tall windows that had been draped in foliage-covered netting. 'They're all dead-ends so far, Sir,' he said. 'But they'll still have to clear them.'

They emerged into a galleried area where an iron staircase spiralled up and down. 'Well, could we put a man down at that end of the corridor so there's a clear field of fire as they come out?' Forsythe asked.

Paddy assessed the situation. 'If you wanted to make it really tough for the attackers, yes, Sir.'

Brucie laughed. 'I do,' he said. 'You heard what the CO said about making the most of it.' Paddy suddenly realized that Brucie needed to shine just as much as he did, or Tony, or any of the men in the cadre. 'Okay,' the Lieutenant said. 'Finish up downstairs and I'll catch up with you there.'

'Sir,' Paddy said. Forsythe had been a lot easier to get along with since Paddy had helped to pull his fat out of the fire at Major Voce's wedding. He might never be Paddy's favourite officer, but at least now they were working together better.

Paddy's boots clattered on the stairs as he went down. He came to the bottom, picked one of the many corridors at random, and found he was in a cul-de-sac. There was an open door to one side, and a door at the end marked 'No Admittance'. Paddy poked his head through the side door, and found a room with no other exits leading off. Then he went to the far door. He knocked on it. No reply. He hesitated for a second, then eased the door open.

What lay beyond was unlike any other room in the whole bare building. It wasn't a large space, but it had been turned into a nice little retreat. There was a desk and an armchair, a fan and three different lamps all blazing away, a coffee percolator and a kettle with several jars of instant and beans and a grinder, a quart jug of milk, a bottle and a half of scotch, a crate of beer, an army-issue pack of toilet rolls, several old ammo cans – Paddy presumed he was using them to store something else – a ghetto blaster with a couple of racks of tapes, and too much other junk for Paddy to work out what it was, all powered by a rat's nest of cabling and extension leads. There was a portable gas heater tucked away in a corner, with a couple of spare cylinders of fuel, and a portable telly perched on a pile of books nearby.

Must be the range warden's place, Paddy decided. All he needs is the cuddly toy, he thought.

He knew Norton – an ex-regimental sergeant major, by all accounts – had been giving Brucie a hard time. Apparently, he'd threatened to shut the exercise down more than once.

Well, Paddy would just have to find a way to make sure that didn't happen. A bit of flattery would probably go a long way. He shut the door and turned, only to see the old man watching him.

'Sergeant?' the old man called. 'Finding your way all right?' He fumbled with a tin of tobacco.

Paddy went up to him. 'I'm sorry, mate,' he said, hoping he hadn't flicked the old man on the raw already. 'I wasn't meaning to pry. I was just doing a recce.'

'You'll have seen the notice then,' Norton asked. Paddy had, of course, but he made a point of letting the old man see him look at it again. 'So that room remains out of bounds for the duration.' Paddy stared at him. He realized Norton wasn't that old – he was maybe in his late fifties, if that. 'Rely on you for that, can I?'

It wasn't very satisfactory, but there were some compromises you had to make. 'Absolutely,' Paddy said. 'I understand completely. It is your place after all.'

'Yes,' the range warden said. He continued to make his roll-up. 'You'd do well to remember that.'

Lieutenant Forsythe came down the stairs and joined them. 'Mr Norton,' he said brightly. 'Everything all right?' He smiled. Paddy suddenly remembered how supremely irritating he'd found that grin when Brucie had first joined the company.

'Yes it will be — if your lads stick to the rules, behave themselves, and don't do any more damage than necessary,' Norton said.

Anyone would think we were a bunch of schoolboys on an outing, Paddy thought. Mind you, looking at Forsythe you had to wonder.

He exchanged a grin with the lieutenant. Norton must have spotted it, because he yelled, 'Then I won't have to stop the exercise, will I?' and dashed away.

Paddy and Forsythe continued checking. Some outing this was going to be, Paddy thought.

A bit later, he'd finished checking, and found the perfect place for their main defence — a top-floor room with two exits and a huge bay window giving an almost two hundred and seventy-degree view of the grounds. He leaned out of it to report to Forsythe.

'This should work fine from here, Sir,' he shouted down to Lieutenant Forsythe. A little way off, Norton stood puffing on one of his roll-ups. He didn't seem happy. 'Do you want to come and have a look?'

'No thank you, Sergeant Garvey,' Forsythe yelled up at him. 'They'll be coming in from over there –' He looked at a stand of trees to the west. 'So you can tape the rest of the area off.'

Paddy got to it, making sure he taped off the end of the cul-de-sac leading to Norton's little home away from home.

Paddy got to the campsite just in time to see Tony and Dave having a bit of a set-to. Tony was playing a game of five-a-side – well, as near as, considering they were using a full water bottle as a ball – and he wanted Dave to join in. But Dave wasn't interested and Tony seemed to be taking it as a personal insult.

Dave rolled up his paper and stuck it into the leg pocket of his combat trousers. He headed away from the others, and when he got to Paddy he seemed set to go straight past.

'Hiya,' Paddy said. 'I was coming to find you.'

'You found me,' Dave said. He didn't seem too thrilled about it.

Paddy pinched his cheek. 'So, how's it going?'

Dave batted his hand away irritably. 'Not now, Paddy,' he said.

'You want to be left alone?' Paddy asked. Stupid question, really, he thought.

'Correct, yes.'

There wasn't much left but to make a joke of it. 'That's fine by me – I never liked you anyway,' Paddy said as he walked away. He decided he was starving and wondered if he could persuade Sally – who was on camp kitchen duty – to rustle him up a bite to eat. He wouldn't have bet his boots on it.

'Oy,' Dave said before he'd got very far. Paddy turned. Dave made a lip-zipping gesture.

'So what is it? Donna?' Paddy asked.

Dave stared at him. He smiled – if you could call an expression where you showed your teeth but looked as if you wanted to cry, a smile. 'How did you know?'

'Well, I didn't think it was a gas bill, did I,' Paddy said. He strolled back to Dave. 'Last time you were like this you thought she was going to walk out on you over that paternity bill.'

Dave looked at his feet. In the distance, the five-a-side hotted up, from the sound of the shouts and jeers. 'Well if she leaves it won't be anything I've done this time.' Dave looked up. There was real desperation in his eyes. He laughed, but the sound was on the verge of a sob. 'I think she's having an affair,' he said.

'Who with?' Paddy said. He'd thought it might be a lot of things, but this had never occurred to him.

'Her college tutor, Mark –' My God, Paddy thought. It was no wonder Dave had taken against her studying. 'Think I've been kidding myself – thinking it's all right, you know. But she's been going to galleries with him, staying late after classes. Then this summer school in Brighton came up –'

'Uh huh,' Paddy said.

'I told her I didn't want her to go. She said I should trust her.' He said it like it was the most outrageous suggestion in the world.

214

'Well, maybe you should,' Paddy said. Dave swallowed, and Paddy realized he was asking too much of his friend. 'Come on, man – you two have been through a lot.' It wouldn't be the first time Donna had played away, and if Dave had never had an affair – to Paddy's knowledge – he'd certainly had enough one-night stands, including a visit or three to the brothels of the world. 'You're still together,' Paddy finished.

Dave considered. 'Aye,' he said. He chewed his lip. 'We haven't had sex since she came back from Brighton.'

'Ouch,' Paddy said. That had been a good month ago.

'The only time she wants to be near me is when she has to be, and then she can't wait to get away again.' It was like the words were being ripped out of him. He smiled again, that dreadful, mirthless smile. 'Might just be the crotch-rot and the piles,' he said. He was closer to tears than laughter. 'Don't think it's that, though.'

What the hell should I say? Paddy wondered. What the hell do you say, when your mate's entire life is coming down around his ears? It wasn't even as if Dave had a brilliant army career to fall back on.

Dave sat down on a pile of kit. 'I don't think it's that,' he said again.

Paddy sat down next to him. Times like this, he wished he still smoked, though he'd finally seen sense on that score. 'Well,' he said, 'it sounds to me like you've just got to ask her.' He shook his head. 'You

215

can't go on like this, mate.' Dave shook his head slightly. Paddy put his hand on his friend's shoulder. 'Come on, Dave,' he urged. 'For all you know it's something completely harmless. Just go out and ask her.'

Dave stared at a spot on the ground. He didn't speak for a long while. Paddy could see a nerve jumping at the corner of his eye. He forced himself to keep quiet. Dave had to sort it out in his own mind.

'What if she says yes?' Dave said at last.

Paddy sucked his teeth. 'That's the risk you take. At least you'll know, hey?' He put a bit of a snap in his voice. 'Otherwise you'll go bloody mad.'

'Yeah. You're right,' Dave said. He didn't sound in the least convinced.

'I think you've got to, mate,' Paddy said. He pounded Dave gently on the back. 'I wouldn't worry about it – it probably is the crotch-rot and the piles.' He didn't believe it for a moment.

He was trying to think what else to say when Tony pounded up and lobbed the water canteen at Dave. He was stripped to the waist and looked fighting fit. Being a father definitely agreed with him.

'Oy,' he said aggressively. Then he switched to a little-boy-lost voice. 'Can I have my ball back please, mister?'

Time to change the subject, Paddy thought. He stripped off his combat jacket. 'What do you reckon,' he hissed at Dave. 'Two against twelve?'

Dave waggled the water bottle. 'Piece of piss,' he said.

They stood up. Paddy glared at Tony. 'Come and get it,' he dared.

'Lads!' Tony called. He beckoned the rest of the men over, at the same time holding his hand out to Paddy and Dave to stay where they were. The men arrived. 'Tournament,' Tony explained to them. He turned back. 'Come on then,' he said to Paddy and Dave.

They walked slowly forward, eyeing the solid wall of flesh in front of them. Paddy glanced at Dave.

Then they charged. Paddy's shoulder hit Tony. He barged the corporal aside, but hands – a lot of hands – grabbed him and he felt himself being dragged under.

Who says sergeants don't have any fun? he thought.

He broke away eventually. Tony grabbed the water canteen and ran with it towards the mess tents. Paddy pounded after him, but just as he caught up Tony lobbed the canteen back to Joe. Then he belted towards the serving tables.

He grabbed the hosepipe out of the hands of the private on clean-up duty, and turned it on Paddy.

'That is very childish,' Paddy said. He waggled a finger at Tony as he walked slowly towards him. At the last minute he darted forward and grabbed the pipe. Dave and Joe leapt in. Tony didn't go down without a struggle, but he did go down. He somehow rolled on the pipe, and water squirted everywhere.

There was a sudden sound of water meeting fabric. 'On your feet,' said an all-too-familiar voice.

Paddy looked up and found himself staring at Major Voce and Colonel Jennings. Water dripped from the colonel's thick black moustache. He scrambled to his feet. So did Dave and Joe, but Tony was still trying to get up when the colonel spoke.

'Good evening, gentlemen,' the colonel said.

'Sir,' they chorused.

'All right, relax,' the colonel said. 'Who's that down there?'

Tony finally got up. Somehow the hosepipe had got stuck between his legs, and he couldn't do anything but stand there with it spraying out water while the colonel spoke to them.

'Corporal Wilton,' said Colonel Jennings. His voice was like the crack of doom. 'Well, I'm glad to see you've all got so much energy left.' He didn't sound glad.

'We were just cooling off, Sir,' Tony said. He laughed in embarrassment.

'Right. Well, don't overdo it,' the colonel said. 'Save something for tomorrow.'

'Sir,' Tony said. 'Uh . . . sorry about the water, Sir.'

'That's quite all right, Corporal Wilton,' Colonel Jennings said. 'Luckily, you missed.' He blew up at his moustache, and droplets of water flew out of it. 'All right – carry on.' He turned and walked away, followed by Major Voce.

They managed not to grin until both the officers had gone. Then they carried on with what they'd been doing. After all, Colonel Jennings had told them to.

A bit later, Paddy walked across to the sergeants' mess tent. CSM Stubbs was there, putting out a folding card table and a couple of chairs.

'You expecting company, Sir?' Paddy asked as he stripped off his soaking tee-shirt. He was hoping to be allowed some free time – it was a beautiful evening, in a beautiful part of the country, and he had a beautiful woman waiting for him.

'Yes,' Stubbs said. He sounded thoroughly pissed off. 'Frank Norton, the range warden. Mr Forsythe is leaning on me to sweeten him up.'

Paddy found a clean tee-shirt. He grinned behind Stubbs' back, realizing he'd just been offered the perfect opening. 'Shall I make myself scarce for a bit, then?' he asked innocently.

'It's up to you, mate,' Stubbs said. 'Don't see the point in both of us suffering, do you?'

Paddy pulled the tee-shirt on. 'Well, I was thinking of taking a little stroll, as it happens.'

Stubbs grinned at him. 'Oh aye? Well, off you go then.'

'Thank you, Sir,' Paddy said, and he walked away, trying to look aimless.

'Give her one for me,' Stubbs said from behind him.

Charming, Paddy thought. He hadn't realized he was that transparent. As he walked over to the catering tents he saw Frank Norton stumping solidly across the grass with his perpetual air of injured innocence almost visible around him.

Paddy found Sally, and they walked to the riverside. He told her about Dave's troubles, and the water fight.

'I really banged my shoulder,' he finished. 'I don't suppose you'd give it a rub would you, Sal?'

'Oh you poor thing,' she said, all mock sympathy. 'Sit yourself down, Sergeant, and I'll see what I can do.'

They found an old tree-root, on a patch of bare ground near the river but shielded from prying eyes by a ring of bushes. Paddy seated himself in front of it, so when Sally sat down she was behind and above him. She started gently enough, but soon she was digging her fingers into the knots that were his back muscles. He groaned.

'No pain, no gain, as we say in aerobics,' Sally said. He could just imagine the smile on her face. She kneaded the back of his neck.

'Uhhh . . .' he muttered. He reached up and guided her hand to the spot below his shoulder blade that was giving him the most trouble. She worked the muscle with deep circular movements of her fingers. It hurt like hell. 'Ah . . .' he said. She pushed harder, sending shafts of pain lancing through him that were somehow still enjoyable. 'Yes . . .' Paddy said. 'Yes . . .' The tension drained out of him.

'I hope no-one's listening in,' Sally said. She eased off the pressure, and the massage became almost restful.

Paddy just lay back and enjoyed it. As he moved back into her hands, he realized that the wet fabric of

220

his combat trousers was chafing at his legs. 'These trousers are all damp, Sal,' he grumbled.

'I'm not quite sure how to take that,' she said. She was still massaging him very gently.

'Eh?' Paddy said, not quite following.

'Paddy, I've been thinking,' she said. Her hands kept working at his back, making it hard for him to concentrate on anything else.

'What have you been thinking?' he asked, hoping they weren't going to have a complicated conversation.

'About this flat of yours,' Sally said.

'What about it?' He wished that, if they were going to have a complicated conversation, she'd stop the massage. As it was, he felt at a distinct disadvantage.

'Well, when you got it, you said you weren't asking me to move in or anything.' She sounded nervous — not at all her usual perky self.

'I wasn't,' Paddy said flatly. He'd been right — the conversation was about to get very complicated.

'Yeah, I know,' she said. He could hear the hurt in her voice.

'Good,' he said, hoping she'd drop the subject. She took her hands off his back, and he knew for sure she was upset. He realized he was going to have to say something, or she'd think he was trying to dump her, and that wasn't any part of his intention. 'Nice though, isn't it — having somewhere we can get away from everyone?'

'Yeah, it is.' Her voice was wistful. 'It's lovely.' She paused, and for a moment he thought he was in the

221

clear. But then she went on, 'And I've been thinking that it seems daft – '

Paddy craned his neck to try and look at her. 'What, love?' he asked, though he knew full well what she was angling at.

'You know – me coming to visit all the time.'

'How d'you mean?' he probed. He didn't want to be at cross purposes with her – maybe if he and Nancy had been better at talking instead of just having fun together, they might have still been together.

'Well . . . what I'm trying to say is . . .' she faltered to a halt. If Paddy hadn't known her better, he would have sworn she sounded scared. She started again. 'I don't mean definitely . . . but if you wanted I could spend a bit more time there.'

For a second Paddy was delighted, just to think she wanted him that much. He twisted round to look at her properly. He'd been right. She looked terrified. And so was he, he realized. 'What?' he asked to buy himself some time. 'You move in with me, you mean?'

'Mmmm,' she said unhappily, obviously sorry she'd started the whole conversation.

'Well . . . that's – ' He'd meant to say, *that's lovely*; but he didn't know if it was or if he was only saying it so as not to hurt her. 'I don't know,' he admitted. 'Are you sure?'

He'd hurt her anyway. 'Not if you don't want to,' she said. 'I just – '

'No,' he said quickly. How could he explain what

222

he meant when he didn't understand it himself? 'I'm not saying I don't want to, Sal. It would be fabulous for us to be together like that. It's just — ' he stopped, completely confused by what he was feeling and the need to choose exactly the right words to explain it.

'What?' she said. Any minute now, she would cry, and if she did that he knew he would promise her anything — even when he knew it was wrong.

'It's just that I don't want to rush in and spoil everything.' Her eyes sparkled in the evening sunlight. 'This is important to me, Sally. You're important to me. I want everything to be right for us. I want us to get to know each other before we make any really big decisions.' He reached forward and hugged her. 'I think it's a really nice idea,' he said. He broke away from her. 'Let's both go away and have a think about it before we make any big decisions.'

'Yeah,' she said.

He stared at her. She was beautiful, and funny, and she loved him. You could lose her, Garvey, he told himself. She's the best thing since —

And then he realized that the end of that sentence was, *Since Nancy*. Since Nancy, but not including her; and all his complicated feelings crystallized in that moment. He knew exactly what his problem was: for all he'd thought he was over Nancy, settling for anyone else felt like settling for second best. He wanted to think he was being noble — that he cared too much for Sally to do that to her.

But he knew that wasn't the problem. The problem was his pride, pure and simple.

When he kissed Sally, he felt like a traitor, and when he said goodnight to her, he felt relieved.

He got back to the sergeants' mess tent just in time to see Frank Norton tottering off in a haze of alcohol.

'Take it easy, Frank,' CSM Stubbs called after him. He hadn't bothered to get up.

'Looks like Mr Forsythe's whisky went down well then,' Paddy said as he watched him go. He went to get his toilet bag. He still felt miserable over Sally, so he decided to pretend he was still on duty – he'd have to cheer up then.

'What a sad man,' the CSM said. 'Hey, Paddy – ' he called over his shoulder, 'you'd better watch out tomorrow, because he's definitely not a lover of our Mr Forsythe, free booze or no free booze.'

You don't say, Paddy thought. But he knew it was a good thing that Stubbs had noticed – it would give him a bit of protection if things went wrong. He picked up a folding chair and went to sit next to the sergeant major.

'Yeah, well,' he said, 'I reckon he's been getting a lot more than the odd bottle of scotch shoved his way.'

'How do you mean, lad?' Stubbs asked.

'He's got a little hideaway in the Fibua building,' Paddy said, keeping his voice low. You never knew who might be listening. He undid the cap of his water bottle, ready to brush his teeth. 'I walked right into it – stashed full of stuff. Packed fuel, compo, the lot.'

Stubbs didn't seem surprised. 'Well, it happens.'

He stood up. 'You know, you might think about that – with your contacts and all.' He slapped Paddy on the shoulder. 'Who's on top tonight?' he asked slyly.

Paddy grinned ruefully. Some chance, with even senior NCOs two to a tent.

Paddy didn't sleep very well that night, but by next morning he'd decided that Sally should never know what he'd discovered by the river. Either they were going to be together, or sooner or later he'd have to leave her – but until that time came, he was going to make her feel like the most important woman in the world.

Which, previous wives excepted, was just what she was.

His first stop that morning was to have a word with Sally. He'd thought about what Stubbs said, and reckoned that since there wasn't an offie nearby, the Catering Corps would have to supply the requisite backhander. It took a bit of sweet talking, but eventually he won a grudging 'Give me ten minutes and I'll see what I can do' out of her.

After that he went to have a word with Tony, who was leading the attack team. His men were prepping in the woods in front of the house – full jungle combats, green camo, and blank firing attachments on their rifles. To his surprise, apart from Tony only one man was fully kitted up – Dave. He stood with his SA80 at the ready, looking for all the world like something out of a recruitment video.

Paddy called Tony over to him. 'You're on the ambush and the Fibua today, right?' Tony nodded. Paddy jerked his head at Dave. 'Well, give him the chance to kick the shit out of something small, will you?'

Tony grinned. 'Trying to win him back off me are you?'

Paddy smiled. 'Just give him a good go, hey?' It was the only thing he could think of that might help.

'Yeah, course I will,' Tony said. 'If he shines, I do.'

So Tony was hot and heavy after his third stripe, Paddy thought. 'Oh out to impress are we?' he said.

Tony was suddenly all seriousness. Sunlight falling through the leaves dappled his face with shadows that added to his camo. 'Course I am, Paddy,' he said. 'Can't pass up on a chance like this, can I?' He gestured at the command centre. 'Got the CO over there watching me. I want to be back in the sergeants' mess, drinking large pints of beer, with or without you, ASAP.' Paddy grinned. One down, two to go: at this rate, they'd all three be back on the rails by Christmas. Tony went on, 'You know if I can get this lot to help me out, I will. Guaranteed.' He grinned. 'See you later.' As Paddy turned and headed towards the catering tents, he heard Tony yell, 'Oy! Maynard! Hurry up will you or you'll be going round the course with my left foot up your arse.'

Paddy grinned. Nothing like a corporal with ambition to keep a bunch of squaddies on their toes.

He wandered over to the catering tents again, trying hard to look like a man with nothing on his mind but a pretty girl. He must have done all right, because the private scrubbing out the stewpot glanced at Sally and then moved away sharpish when he saw Paddy.

'Hiya,' he said. He thought, she is beautiful. I must be crazy to think she's second-best. It was just that when he looked at her he kept remembering a woman with darker hair and a throaty chuckle. He put that out of his mind. 'Did you get it?' he asked, as if he were talking about the weather. He stood cradling his helmet in his arms, feeling as conspicuous as a white cat on a black night.

'Stealing rations is a court-martial offence, or didn't you know?' Sally asked.

'Oh come on, Sal. No-one's going to notice one jar and a few rashers of bacon,' he said. He felt like he were using her. It was only the fact that he was pretty certain she was just winding him up, and that he really was doing it for the platoon, that kept him from saying as much. 'Just pretend it got lost in transit.'

'All right for you to say,' Sally grumbled. 'What do you want them for, anyway?'

'Trust me,' Paddy said, tapping his nose. 'It's all in a good cause.' She looked at him sceptically. 'You look fantastic in khaki,' he said with a lecherous grin. That much at least was true.

'Oh shut up,' Sally said, but she was already heading into the provisions tent.

Paddy unslung his pack, so when she came out with a jar of coffee and a pack of bacon he was ready to slide them inside. 'You are top babe,' he said, and for that one second, he meant it.

Just as he swung the pack up on his shoulder, CSM Stubbs came over. 'Come on, leave each other alone, you two,' he called. When he got closer, he said, 'Paddy, did you –'

Paddy patted his pack. 'Yes, Sir. It's all fixed.'

Sally looked hard at him. She was obviously putting two and two together and making twenty-two, Paddy thought. He was surprised when the next thing Stubbs said was, 'Sar'nt Hawkins, how do you feel like playing at real soldiers this morning?'

'Sir?' Sally said, surprised.

'Mr Forsythe's in charge of the enemy forces – hard to believe, I know – and one of his lads's gone down with the plague, and I suggested you as a replacement.'

'Yeah! Sir, I'd love it,' Sally said.

'Sally!' Paddy said, shocked. He turned hurriedly to Stubbs. 'I mean, what about the colour sergeant, Sir?'

'Gone back to barracks with the walking wounded,' he said. He's enjoying this, Paddy thought. 'I'm sorry, Sar'nt Garvey, but Mr Forsythe doesn't have any choice.'

Paddy tried one more time. 'But Sergeant Hawkins hasn't trained –'

'Paddy!' Sally said. 'I'll be ready in five minutes, Sir.' She disappeared into the catering tent.

Paddy stood squinting into the sunlight, feeling pissed off and particularly stupid. This is just what I did with Nance, he thought. She might be a cook but making chips isn't the limit of what she wants. If I'm going to keep her, I'd better remember that.

'Don't worry, mate, she'll be fine,' Stubbs said. It was true, Paddy realized. After all, how much trouble could anyone get into when it wasn't even a live firing exercise. 'As for Mr Forsythe, I think he's about to have a fit. Go and calm him down will you? He's over there by the trucks, playing with his sandbags.'

'Yes, Sir,' Paddy said. Suddenly, he felt as confused as he ever had. He wanted Sally, but he knew he had to stop comparing her with Nancy. So how come, the one way in which they were really similar – wanting to get on in the army – was the one where he most wished they were different?

As it turned out, Brucie had plenty to have a fit about. Norton hadn't turned up, and the front door of the mansion was padlocked.

As Paddy rounded the corner of the building, the lieutenant pounded on the chipboard with which the door had been boarded up. 'Mr Norton,' he screamed at the building.

I'd lay odds he isn't in there, Paddy thought as he got to the back of the truck. I bet he's got a crib some-where far enough away that he can't be found when he doesn't want to be.

Sally jumped out first, before Paddy could stop her. He put his hand up to the rest. 'All right lads – stay where you are.'

'Any sign of him?' Brucie asked.

'I'm afraid not, Sir – there's a couple of doors round the back, but they're both boarded up.' He hesitated. 'We could do this lock for you, Sir, if you wanted – if you don't mind the damage.'

Brucie sighed. 'All right, Sar'nt. Break it open. We'll worry about Mr Norton as and when.'

'Sir,' Paddy said. 'Sal – ' He couldn't bring himself to call her by her surname. 'Can you get us something for this?' He went to examine the lock. It was a simple hasp and padlock, more of a formality than a security device.

Sally handed him a tyre iron. 'Here you go,' she said.

Paddy hooked the end of the iron under the hasp and applied a bit of pressure. The hasp popped off the door, and they were in.

They went inside and Paddy deployed the men according to the plan he and Forsythe had worked out earlier. He considered tucking Sally away somewhere out of harm's way, but he knew she'd give him grief for it. Besides, he intended to spend most of his time, at least to begin with, on the main gun emplacement overlooking the front door, so he assigned her there – it kept her happy and at least he could keep an eye on her.

He put her to work shifting sandbags – give her a taste of the man's life in the modern army, he decided, just like it said in the glossy recruiting videos.

'See Sal?' he asked as he lounged up against the wall. 'It's not all tearing round with guns.' She didn't answer, just picked up another sandbag and piled it on the others against the window wall, to make a machine-gun emplacement. 'Want a hand?' he asked, wondering what it would take to get her to admit she couldn't cope.

'Don't even think about it,' she said. 'I've lifted bigger bags of flour.' She stacked the bag. 'Hope your attacking section's in good shape,' she said.

'Oh — feeling tough, are we?' Paddy asked.

'Going to make the most of this,' Sally said. That's what I'm afraid of, Paddy thought. He could see her running riot through Brucie's carefully planned defences. 'After all, I don't get many chances to shoot Dave Tucker and Tony Wilton, do I?' She looked up at him. He couldn't honestly say her camo suited her, but somehow her combats managed to accentuate her curves. She shifted the last sandbag. 'Just a shame you're not part of the attack yourself,' she said thoughtfully. She picked up her SA80. 'Give you a chance to see what living with me might be like.'

She walked off before Paddy could answer, which was just as well since he couldn't think of anything to say. He decided he'd better check out the other assignments. For once in a wonder, they were all fine. By the time he got back, Sally and Knox had finished building the gun emplacement in front of the net-and-foliage draped window. She was squatting in front of the sandbags, and Knox was showing her how the ammo belt fed through the machine gun. She closed the casing and settled the stock of the gun against her shoulder. For a second, he considered ordering them to swap places. Then he decided, to hell with it. Why spoil her fun? He'd already lost one woman with his fixed opinions of what a woman's place was. He'd be damned if he'd make it two.

'Don't worry,' he said. 'They'll be another ten minutes yet.'

Sally grinned at him. 'I told you – it's them that's got to worry.'

Paddy settled himself on the sandbags. 'Yeah, well – just remember, if you're in a room and a grenade comes in, or you get caught in a line of fire, you're dead. Okay?' He paused for emphasis. 'No cheating.'

'As if I would,' Sally said. She grinned impishly. 'Can't have your boys shown up by a girl, can we?'

Chance'd be a fine thing, Paddy thought, but he didn't say anything. Before he could continue his little lecture, he heard voices shouting outside. He looked through the window. Norton was haranguing Brucie.

'Oh shit,' Paddy said. 'I've got to go – see you later.'

He raced downstairs. By the time he got outside to the truck, Norton was threatening to close the exercise down – and as range warden, he was within his rights to do so.

Paddy trotted up to them, and didn't bother waiting for Forsythe to acknowledge him. ''Scuse me, Sir,' he said without preamble. 'I think you need to go and check out the new gun position.' He pointed at the upstairs bay window, hoping that Stubbs had told Brucie of their plan, the way he had promised to.

Brucie sighed. 'Give me a moment, Sergeant Garvey,' he said.

'It's very important, Sir,' Paddy said. 'In fact it's quite urgent.' He tried to drop Forsythe the nod without Norton noticing it, but the lieutenant was far too wound up to get it, so Paddy continued, 'And I'd

232

quite like to have a little chat with Mr Norton myself, if that's possible.'

Forsythe sighed again. 'All right – and be quick about it. I have to go and meet the first section.' He left at a trot.

'Bloody schoolboys,' Norton snarled as soon as he'd gone.

'Yeah, I know,' Paddy said. 'They just never listen, but what can you do?'

'Well, he should have listened to me this time,' Norton said. His face was flushed and he was breathing hard. 'I'll have him for breaking in like that – I'll close him down, I will –'

This is the tricky bit, Paddy thought. 'Ah,' he said. 'Now that actually was my suggestion.' He watched Norton's face closely, but the older man was lost in his anger and didn't seem to notice. 'You see I knew that you and Sar'nt Major Stubbs had been on the sauce last night –' that was good, he knew – let an army man take some of the blame. ' – and I figured you might be a bit late for work this morning.' Norton looked at him sharply. 'But don't worry about the lock – I'll get it sorted, okay?' He hurried on so as not to give Norton a chance to interrupt. 'Oh, and I've taped off the area round your room, so nobody's going to bother you there.' He paused.

Norton had had the wind taken out of his sails, but only for a minute. He took a deep breath and said, 'Yeah but even so that –'

'And,' Paddy said, playing his hole card, 'I thought I'd bring you a little something for the morning after.'

He unslung his pack and let Norton have a peek inside at the coffee and bacon. 'Got a friend in the cookhouse, you see,' he explained, knowing Norton would think the food tasted finer if it had been liberated from the army. 'So what do you say?' he asked. 'Shall we have a quick cup of tea?'

Norton clapped him on the shoulder. 'Now you're talking,' he said. He obviously thought he'd found a kindred spirit, whereas Paddy found his dislike of the man growing moment by moment.

He followed Norton inside. They went to the cramped little cubbyhole Paddy had found the day before, and he let the man make him a cup of tea. Norton also put some of the bacon on to fry – he had a little Baby Belling stove tucked away in a corner – and the smell made Paddy wish he could stay long enough to have some, even if it did mean talking to Norton.

He cleared a stack of magazines off a tea chest and sat down. He took a long sip of tea, wondering how soon he could get away without pissing the old man off.

'So,' Norton said. 'How long you been with the regiment then, Paddy?'

Garvey considered. 'Too long,' he said, knowing it would please Norton even though he didn't really mean it. 'Twelve years nearly, now.'

Norton harumphed. 'Long enough to remember things when they were done properly, then.' He pronounced the words very carefully, and Paddy wondered exactly what he'd put in his cup. 'None of this poncy new thinking like they've got now,' he said. 'Glad I got out when I did,' he shouted.

'Yeah, you've really landed on your feet here, haven't you?' Paddy said, making a show of looking round at the room, with its chaotic treasure trove of bribes and knockbacks and found items. 'Nice little set up,' Paddy said approvingly.

'Perks of the job,' Norton said proudly. It was hard to imagine him as a regimental sergeant major – but not at all hard to imagine why he'd been turned down for a late entry commission, as CSM Stubbs had told Paddy he had been. 'When your Mr Forsythe's learned a bit more – if ever he does – he'll find out there are ways and ways of getting a job done – know what I mean.'

Paddy stared at him levelly, unwilling to agree yet not daring to disagree. Norton reached over and rummaged in a desk drawer. He came up with a rather nice silver and leather hip-flask, which he brandished at Paddy. 'Want a pick me up for that?' he asked.

'No, no,' Paddy said. 'I'm fine, thanks.' There were limits to what he was prepared to do to keep the exercise on the rails, and being caught drinking on duty overstepped them.

Norton settled himself in his easy chair, apparently ready to continue the conversation, but Paddy was saved by the rattle of gunfire from outside. 'Shit!' he said. He leaped up and grabbed his helmet. 'They've already started. I'd better get out there.' He was across the room in a couple of strides.

'Got to hold Mr Forsythe's hand, eh?' Norton said as Paddy left the room. 'Come again, mate?'

Paddy turned. It had to be worth the extra couple of seconds to keep him sweet. 'Yeah,' he said. 'Thanks, mate.'

He closed the door behind him, ran down the corridor and ducked under the tape at the mouth of the cul-de-sac just in time to bump into Lieutenant Forsythe.

'You sort him?' the officer asked.

'I think so, Sir,' Paddy replied as he put on his helmet. 'He shouldn't bother us for a while now, anyway.' He tightened his chin-strap.

'Brilliant! Thank you,' Forsythe said; and Paddy thought, Norton's wrong. Brucie's come a long way since he joined us. 'Right,' the lieutenant continued. 'Fire position first floor – I'm going up to the balcony.' He didn't wait for Paddy to respond, but turned and ran up the ornate central staircase. Paddy followed.

Gunfire and the sound of feet pounding on bare floorboards came from upstairs. If they'd done what Paddy anticipated, they'd shimmied up to one of the top balconies on ropes, and now they'd be working their way down, clearing rooms as they went. Sure enough, he saw shadowy movement in the stairwell above him as he took the steps three at a time. Smoke from thunderflashes was starting to drift down, and every so often he heard someone yell, 'Grenade!' The things didn't go off – you just accepted that if you could see one, you were dead.

He got to the machine-gun emplacement just in time to meet Sally leaving the room. She'd run out of ammo, and equipped herself with an SA80 instead.

'Where are you going?' he demanded.

'Making a counter attack,' she said, as if it were the most natural thing in the world. 'I told you — I'm going to make the most of this.'

He watched her from the doorway for a minute. She found a corner where she could cover a small side staircase. It went up, turned on itself and ended at a cross corridor; an open door led into a room immediately opposite the mouth of the staircase. Shouts and gunfire rang out from the cross corridor. Feet slammed on the wooden floors. He saw her run halfway up the first flight of stairs and let loose with her SA80. Joe Farrell said something incomprehensible, and he heard Dave yell something else. She dived back down and got into cover safely.

Paddy realized with some amusement that she'd managed to get half of Tony's mob penned up. Damn, he thought. She's actually good at this. He crept out to join her. She let loose another burst. It was answered by several weapons. Tony said something, but it was impossible to tell what. Then he and Dave leaned over and filled the stairwell with gunfire.

'Now what?' he whispered. He suddenly realized that he was about to take tactical advice from a cook. It bothered him less than he might have expected.

'Strategic withdrawal,' she hissed back. She dodged down the corridor. Paddy decided not to follow her — he needed to check out what was going on elsewhere. The exercise hadn't been designed to let the defenders win unless the attackers cocked up completely, but he wanted to put on the best show he could.

From behind him he heard Tony yell, 'Grenade!'

The next second Sally called out, in a fair imitation of an American accent, 'They got me, Sarge. They got me –' and she made a horrible strangling noise. Paddy grinned. Making the most of it, indeed.

Mind you, she'd lasted a damned sight longer than most of his lads, by the look of it.

Suddenly he heard Norton yell, 'Oh bloody hell!' and then, 'There's a fire down here, lads.'

'Stand firm,' he heard Tony call.

Norton's cubbyhole, he thought. It was the only place it could possibly be. 'End ex,' he shouted as he ran. 'End ex!'

He thundered down the main stairs and into the main corridor. Norton was staggering along under the weight of a fire extinguisher. Tony came down the side stairs and cut in front of Paddy. He ran after Norton.

Paddy followed them. He came to the mouth of the cul-de-sac. Flames were licking up from under the cubbyhole door. Dave was a little way into the passage. Norton and Tony were almost at the door, silhouetted by the orange light. The smoke made Paddy's eyes water and his throat burn. He ducked under the tape, but even as he did so Tony grabbed the old man, who began to struggle.

'My stuff,' Norton shouted. 'My stuff.' He lashed out. The door sprang open.

The next instant, the cul-de-sac was engulfed in a ball of flame. Paddy got his arms up in front of his face as the heat drove him back.

He heard Tony give one high-pitched scream. Then he was silent.

Later, Paddy and Dave sat on the grass outside the mansion. People said things to them. Paddy heard things. An electrical fault. Illegal supplies. No shadow of blame.

But most of all he heard the voice in his head that said over and over again, Tony's dead, Tony's dead, Tony's dead.

No shadow of blame. Colonel Jennings had said that to him. Was saying it, probably, even now, to someone. But he was wrong.

Tony was dead and it was Paddy's fault, because he had seen the mess of a cubbyhole. He'd been so proud of the way he got round Norton, when he should have been insisting the whole sorry rats' nest of a place was cleaned out.

But even that didn't matter. Tony was dead.

# Chapter 11

They gave Tony a soldier's funeral: his mates to carry his coffin, with his cap on top of it, and three volleys from a dozen rifles to mark his passing.

It wasn't enough. How could it ever be enough, Paddy wondered.

It was the first time he'd ever cried in front of his mates. He hoped it would be the last.

They got drunk, of course, him and Dave together. And for every pint they sank, they left one on the bar for Tony.

After that there was just a long succession of grey days, in which he did his job and that was all. He barely spoke to anyone. Not to Sally, though she left a note to phone her pinned to his door; and not to Dave, whose bad time with Donna had intensified to the point where he was barely functional.

CSM Stubbs and Mr Forsythe came to him. They asked him to nominate someone to be Sentry – the central position – at the Ceremony of the Keys, a very big event for Four Platoon.

'Tucker,' he said, and when they said he was a bad choice, Paddy insisted. The poor bastard had to have something to hang on to.

One night, he was sitting alone, flipping through his photo collection: Tony and him in Hong Kong, Tony in Sarajevo, in New Zealand and in Ulster. All gone, all gone, never to come again. He'd have given everything he had – maybe not Sally, but then he was no longer sure if he had her anyway – but every single other thing to have one of those times again.

There was a knock at the door. Sally, he thought. Sally!

He went to answer it. Mrs Voce – Captain Butler as she had been – was standing there. He tried hard not to let his disappointment show.

'Hello, Ma'am,' he said.

'Hello Sergeant Garvey,' she said. 'I know this is a bit unusual – '

'But very nice of course,' he cut in. He was only glad of the company.

'Of course!' she agreed. 'Well, can I come in?'

He showed her through into the living room. He suddenly realized there was dirty underwear all over the sofa. He grabbed the clothes, apologizing furiously.

'Did you think I was going to be Sergeant Hawkins?' Captain Voce asked.

'No!' he lied. She grinned at him. 'Yes,' he admitted.

She wandered round in front of the sofa. 'This is lovely,' she said. 'Did you do it yourself or was it her?'

'Bit of both,' he said. He felt terribly awkward. 'But mostly me.' He sighed. 'I'm sorry. I'm a bit all over the place. Do you want a drink?'

241

'I'd love one,' Captain Voce said. She smiled, and it lit up her face.

He offered her a choice of beer or wine. She chose wine, and when he brought it through she said, 'Major Voce is off to Camberley and I thought I'd take the opportunity to see how you are – and to say goodbye.'

'Oh?' Paddy said, before he remembered. 'That's right, Ma'am – you're off on your sunshine posting, aren't you?'

'That's right,' she said as she took her glass from him. 'Three months in Belize.'

'That'll be a bit tough on you and Major Voce, won't it?' he asked; he thought, if I were him I don't think I could stand to be parted from her for three weeks, let alone three months.

'I know,' she said. 'Still, I remember what you told me in Cyprus.' She sat down on the sofa, next to the photos. 'Hold on to what you love.' Paddy didn't know what to say to that. But Captain Voce had spotted the photos. She picked one up. 'Oh – our terrible trio,' she said. 'You're going to miss him, aren't you?'

'Yes,' Paddy said. 'Always.' His eyes were burning. He sat down heavily in the armchair. 'I can't stop thinking about it,' he said. 'I know at the end I was a sergeant and Tony was the corporal, but that wasn't right –' he shook his head.

'What do you mean?'

'What I mean is –' he paused, trying to think of words to explain. 'If he'd been running that exercise, I don't think that accident would have happened.'

Captain Voce shook her head, making her dark hair catch the light. 'That's just not true,' she protested.

'I was in Norton's room at the range. I saw all the gear he had.' He'd thought about it over and over again, and he was sure he was right. 'Now, I had the chance to realize what could've happened.' He swallowed hard. His throat was tight. He'd never told this to anyone, outside of the official enquiry. 'If I'd been awake, I would've.' He stopped. There was only one link left in the chain of his logic. 'Tony Wilton would've been awake.'

'I read the report, Sar'nt Garvey, in which you are completely exonerated,' she insisted. 'No-one could've anticipated that fire.'

Paddy wasn't having it. 'All the equipment was staring me in the face.'

But then, neither was Captain Voce. 'Tony Wilton's death was an accident, and if anyone was to blame, it was Norton.' She stared at her wine. 'God knows he paid the price.'

Paddy tried to smile, but he just couldn't make it work. 'It's thrown me,' he said. 'It really has.' He tried again. 'I mean, I know we're soldiers. Used to death — supposed to be — but to die like that . . . for what?'

Captain Voce couldn't look at him. 'Have you talked to Sally?'

She probably thinks she's on to a safe subject, Paddy thought. 'Uhh . . . I think that's part of the problem.' He ran his hand through his hair. 'I wanted to talk to her, but when it came to it, I didn't.' He stopped. 'I couldn't.' And stopped again. 'I haven't seen her since the funeral.'

'Do you really like her?' Captain Voce asked. Paddy thought, well yes; but he was glad she'd said like and not love – that would have been a much harder question to answer. But Captain Voce went on, 'Or are you just worried about ending up unattached and propping up the bar in the sergeants' mess?'

'Yeah,' Paddy was surprised to hear himself say. 'I'm worried about that, and I want kids.' It sounded so honest, yet he knew there was one thing he had to say. 'It's Nance,' he added eventually. 'It's crazy! I've done it a couple of times now. I get to a certain stage with someone and then I start comparing them to Nancy.'

Captain Voce looked sad and a bit bewildered, which was pretty much the way Paddy felt. 'Do you think Sally knows this?' she asked.

'No, I don't think so,' Paddy said. He certainly hoped not.

Captain Voce leaned forward. 'Well, maybe you should be honest with her,' she said. 'Talk to her.' She smiled. 'You did it so well for me when I couldn't see where I was going or what I was doing.' Paddy just stared at her. He couldn't imagine doing what she was suggesting. 'Just talk to her,' she begged him. 'Then if it doesn't work out, at least you'll know –' Now where have I heard that one before? Paddy thought. ' – you won't be left with a nagging question for the rest of your life.'

'Yes,' he said slowly. 'I think you're right.'

After that, things seemed to come back into focus a bit, though he couldn't quite get the nerve up to ring Sally.

The next day, Four Platoon went on a training run. Dave looked terrible, and he could barely keep up with the rest of the men.

'How you doing, Dave?' Paddy asked as they jogged through the woods. No answer. 'Have you spoken to Donna?' No answer. Paddy was beginning to get seriously worried. 'Dave man – answer me!' he said. Still no answer.

They came to a log, which every man in front of them had jumped on and off without incident. Paddy stuck his leg out as Dave leaped down. Dave went down hard, and before he could get his breath back Paddy planted his knee in the other man's back. 'Shut up and stay there,' he said. He pulled Dave's leg back by the ankle, stripped off his trainer and sock and made a great show of examining his foot. 'He's turned his ankle, Sir,' he yelled in reply to Forsythe's enquiry. 'I'd better take him back to the barracks.'

'Can you walk, Tucker?' Forsythe asked.

'I think so, Sir,' Dave replied from his position face-down in the mulch.

'Carry on, Sergeant Garvey,' Lieutenant Forsythe said.

'Sir!' Paddy said. He waited for the platoon to get out of earshot, then said, 'Right. Now talk to me.'

They found a place to sit in the shadow of a big oak tree.

'Well, I asked her,' Dave said. 'It was better not knowing. Can't hide from it now.' He shredded a bit of leaf between his fingers. 'She wants somebody else.'

'You don't know that for sure,' Paddy said. It sounded hollow even to his own ears, but what else could he say?

'No?' Dave asked. He didn't sound as if it had given him hope. 'She said she loved him. Loved him.' His eyes glistened with tears. 'I keep seeing that corridor in the training camp,' he said, and at first Paddy thought he was trying to change the subject, but he went on, 'Me and Tony running down it. I wish I'd beaten him to that door,' he said. He sounded like his heart was breaking. 'I really do.'

'Don't be bloody stupid, Dave,' Paddy said.

'I'm not being stupid, Paddy, I'm being *right*!' Dave shouted.

'That's bollocks, Dave.'

'I thought about it last night,' Dave said. 'It should have been my funeral. Then it would have read: *Here lies Dave Tucker, crap soldier*.' He stopped speaking. Paddy let the silence last for as long as he needed it. 'Then you would have been sad, and Donna would have cried a bit. Gone off with her bloke.' He grinned, suddenly. 'And I'd be up in heaven, getting extra drill from St Peter.'

'Heaven's a bit ambitious for you, isn't it?' Paddy asked. He couldn't bear to see his mate like this, but he thought he couldn't go far wrong with a joke.

But Dave started to cry, almost. 'I don't know what

I'm doing,' he said. 'This was the one thing I got right. Marrying Donna. Having Macaulay.'

Christ, he's given up, Paddy thought. 'Dave, mate – don't do this,' Paddy said. He put a bit of snap into his voice. 'Come on.'

Dave did cry then. 'I don't know what I'm going to do,' he said.

'Fight for her,' Paddy said.

'How?' Dave asked. His voice was thick with despair.

Paddy didn't have an answer. 'I don't know. Anyway you can. Anything.' He thought about it. 'Listen, Dave, Donna's not going to walk out on you just like that. Not with Macaulay.' Dave stared at him. He was calmer now. 'If she was going to, she'd have done it already. Fight for her, Dave.' He could only think of one other thing to say. 'Like Tony would have. Like he did when he nearly lost Joy.' He was wrong. There was one more thing. 'Like I never did, with Nance.' Captain Voce had said he was good at talking to people. Dave might not be crying any more, but he wasn't okay. You only had to look in his eyes to know that. 'Dave, Donna's not gone yet. She's confused. She doesn't know what to do. Help her with that.' Dave didn't respond. 'Help her make her mind up.' Still no response. 'You two,' Paddy said gently. 'You go together. You were made for each other.'

And now Dave did respond. 'Yeah,' he said. 'We're the perfect couple, aren't we?'

'No, I never said that,' Paddy dead-panned. He waited for a sharp comeback. There wasn't one. He got to his feet. 'Come on,' he said. He gave Dave a hand up.

'Thank you Doctor Ruth,' Dave said. He laughed.

Then suddenly they were hugging each other. Dave pulled away. 'Tony's dead,' he said, as if he'd only just heard.

'I know,' Paddy said quietly. And after that they didn't say anything for a long while, because what was there to say?

Paddy lay on the sofa listening to the CD player he'd been given in Cyprus. He and Dave had borrowed Joe's car and gone to see Tony's grave, but it hadn't helped. Nothing helped.

Paddy had dropped Dave off at the married quarters. The very last thing he'd said to him had been, 'Remember what I said – fight for her.' Then he'd come home.

Within an hour Dave had phoned to say that Donna had announced that she was leaving. Paddy had told him to come round, and he'd said he would – but he never showed up, and Paddy was scared to go out looking for him in case he missed him.

So he dozed on the sofa. A touch on his chest roused him. He opened his eyes. Sally stood looking down at him. 'Hiya,' he said.

'Hi,' she said. She didn't smile.

'I got your message,' he said.

'Good,' she said. She walked round to the front of the sofa. Paddy took his headphones off and sat up. 'Phone out of order, was it?' she asked. She sat down next to him.

248

'No, it wasn't,' he said. She looked hurt. It was an expression he was far too used to seeing lately. 'I'm sorry, Sally,' he said. It sounded pathetic. 'How are you? How've you been?'

'Getting by,' she answered. She hesitated. 'Paddy – remember what we said? On the exercise? About living together?'

'Yes,' he whispered.

'And?'

'I don't know, Sal,' he said. He didn't want to hurt her; but he knew he didn't have anything to put into a relationship at the moment. 'I can't seem to think as far ahead as that at the moment.'

'What's going on?' she asked. It was on the tip of his tongue to say that Tony's death had knocked him back, but he didn't want to use that as an excuse. 'I was there too, Paddy, when he died,' she said. 'One minute we were joking around. Then he was gone.' She glared at him. 'So I'm hurting too.' They stared at each other. It was the first time they'd argued – really argued, not just playing. 'You can't have all the grief to yourself,' she said.

'I don't want it,' Paddy answered.

She smiled. It wasn't much of a smile, but it was there all the same. 'Then like I said – call me.' She leaned over and kissed him lightly on the lips. Then, without another word, she got up and walked out.

He didn't turn to watch her go, but he heard her footsteps and when she got to the door he said, 'Sal?' She stopped. 'How long have I got?'

'Five seconds,' she said. 'Five weeks. As long as you need.' Then she walked out the door.

She's going, he thought. No matter what she says, she won't be there if I let her go now. Nancy's gone, he thought. Nancy's the past. I can live in the past or I can live now, because pretty soon they could be carrying me off in a wooden box and firing a few guns for me, and that'll be the end of Paddy Garvey.

'Sally!' he shouted. He rolled off the sofa, and crossed the room in two strides. He got to the hall just as she was opening the front door. 'Sally, come back,' he begged.

She shut the door softly, and let him pull her into his arms, and then there was at least one thing in the world to hold on to.

# BROOKSIDE –
# THE EARLY YEARS

* Revised and updated edition of the original
  *Brookside: The First Ten Years*

* Publication to coincide with the transmission of
  'Brookside: The Early Years' on UK Living

* Chronicles the background of the series, its
  original aims and its evolution over the first
  decade

* Includes a month-by-month plot summary of the
  first ten years

* All the characters are featured – from the Grants
  and the Collinses to the Corkhills and the Dixons

* Individual profiles of the characters and
  interviews with the cast members

* Illustrated with photographs of the characters
  and memorable moments from the early years

Geoff Tibballs
0 7522 1051 3
£7.99 pb

# OTHER TV TIE-IN TITLES AVAILABLE FROM BOXTREE

| | | |
|---|---|---|
| ☐ 0 7522 1051 3 | Brookside: The Early Years | £7.99 pb |
| ☐ 0 7522 0846 2 | Brookside: The Jimmy Corkhill Story | £4.99 pb |
| ☐ 0 7522 0972 8 | Brookside: The Journals of Beth Jordache | £4.99 pb |
| ☐ 0 7522 0765 2 | Brookside: Beth Jordache – The New Journals | £4.99 pb |
| ☐ 0 7522 0984 1 | Between the Lines: Tony Clark's Dossier | £9.99 pb |
| ☐ 1 85283 964 3 | The Bill: The First Ten Years | £9.99 pb |
| ☐ 1 85283 959 7 | Emmerdale Family Album | £9.99 pb |
| ☐ 0 7522 0632 X | Eurotrash: A Weird Guide to Europe | £10.99 pb |
| ☐ 1 85283 498 6 | Food File | £8.99 pb |
| ☐ 1 85283 477 3 | Great Commanders | £12.99 pb |
| ☐ 0 7522 1070 X | Heartbeat: The Real Life Story | £9.99 pb |
| ☐ 0 7522 1000 9 | Intensive Care | £9.99 pb |
| ☐ 1 85283 942 2 | It's a Vet's Life | £8.99 pb |
| ☐ 1 85283 947 3 | Labours of Eve | £8.99 pb |
| ☐ 1 85283 907 4 | Life and Times of the Rovers Return | £9.99 pb |
| ☐ 1 85283 874 4 | London's Burning | £9.99 pb |
| ☐ 1 85283 938 4 | Making of Peak Practice | £9.99 pb |
| ☐ 1 85283 471 4 | On Call with Dr Finlay | £9.99 pb |
| ☐ 1 85283 928 7 | On Duty with The Chief | £9.99 pb |
| ☐ 0 7522 0750 4 | Soldier Soldier: Tucker's Story | £4.99 pb |
| ☐ 0 7522 1075 0 | Taggart Casebook: The First Ten Years | £9.99 pb |
| ☐ 0 7522 1001 7 | Wycliffe | £10.99 pb |

*All these books are available at your local bookshop or can be ordered direct from the publisher. Just tick the titles you want and fill in the form below.*

Prices and availability subject to change without notice.

---

Boxtree Cash Sales, P.O. Box 11, Falmouth, Cornwall TR10 9EN

Please send a cheque or postal order for the value of the book and add the following for postage and packing:

U.K. including B.F.P.O. – £1.00 for one book plus 50p for the second book, and 30p for each additional book ordered up to a £3.00 maximum.

Overseas including Eire – £2.00 for the first book plus £1.00 for the second book, and 50p for each additional book ordered.

OR please debit this amount from my Access/Visa Card (delete as appropriate).

Card Number

| | | | | | | | | | | | | | | | |
|---|---|---|---|---|---|---|---|---|---|---|---|---|---|---|---|

Amount £ .........................................................................................

Expiry Date .....................................................................................

Signed ..............................................................................................

Name ................................................................................................

Address ............................................................................................